Laura Dickey

Autobiography of Mrs. Laura Dickey

Laura Dickey

Autobiography of Mrs. Laura Dickey

ISBN/EAN: 9783337027995

Printed in Europe, USA, Canada, Australia, Japan

Cover: Foto ©Raphael Reischuk / pixelio.de

More available books at **www.hansebooks.com**

AUTOBIOGRAPHY

OF

MRS. LAURA DICKEY

AND

Choice Miscellaneous Selections

CHICAGO, ILL.

CHAPMAN PUBLISHING CO.

1895.

Preface

AS one of the pioneers of Chicago, having come here in October, 1846, this short sketch of my life I would dedicate to those ladies of the city who for many successive years — in connection with taking **FAITH'S RECORD** — have treated me with marked courtesy and kindness, and have manifested the amount of interest in my personal history which encourages this effort to reproduce some of the incidents connected with a long, active, and not altogether uneventful, life.   L. D.

INDEX.

CHAPTER FIRST.

MY EARLY LIFE.

I WAS born September 27, 1811, in the town of Newstead, Erie County, N. Y., where my parents, Samuel and Jane Anderson, settled in their early married life. There, surrounded by broad acres, with everything additional which their thrift and industry could acquire, I was reared in a home of plenty, free from all anxiety and care; for my mother—wonderful woman that she was—seemed more than competent to assume all responsibility. I can scarcely find words in which to express all the admiration I felt for her in those childish days, or even that which her memory elicits at this late date. Generous to a fault, firm yet affectionate, not only to her own, but to every needy one who came within the radius of her influence, she proved a friend and benefactor. The memory of such a mother has proved a life-long blessing, and that early beautiful past has always seemed to me like an oasis in the desert in life's wearisome hours. I had a kind, indulgent father, and all that was ever expected of Lottie, as I was affectionately called—my name being Laura—was to look after my younger brothers and sisters, and this was to me only a labor of love. I have sometimes thought the knowledge thus obtained, as it regarded the care of little ones, together with my natural love for children, combined, in after years, to decide what my vocation should be when circumstances threw me upon my own resources. Much as I love to linger on this blissful period of my life, even as the happy years so quickly fled, I, too, must hasten in their review.

While very young, I was married to the man of my choice, and though as time went by I was both wife and mother, still I knew no care, for my mother, knowing how incompetent I was to take charge of a house, and my

husband (well pleased at my freedom from care), arranged that we should
board at my father's. And so the happy hours flew by, until the loss of my
husband enveloped me in such a cloud of darkness and despair, that, nearly
bereft of reason, I was considered incapable of giving necessary attention
to my two babies (the eldest not being two years old). In looking back
to those dark days life for many months seemed only a blank; but God
is good, making youth elastic, and time a restorer. Again I married, and
shortly afterward we moved to Canada, where Mr. Balch, my husband's
father, lived. I will not dwell on this time of my life, only to say I there
began to learn what life really was in its labors and responsibilities. I had
never before known the real value of money, in fact I had almost everything
to learn, but the many, and sometimes bitter, lessons were as nothing when
compared to the terrible home-sickness I experienced at the separation from
home and friends, and to attempt a description of my feelings at that time
would prove fruitless, except in one definite, ever-present thought, which
amounted to a longing for that religion of which I had heard so many speak,
but of which I had no personal knowledge. My prayer was, "Father in
heaven, what must I do to be saved? I believe in Christ as my Savior, and
I pray that Thou wilt give me the evidence of sins forgiven." But, though
I prayed most fervently, I never could feel the assurance of acceptance, so
I thought I had only to wait, and in His own good time He would send
the same evidence to my waiting spirit that others had spoken of receiving.
Thus I waited and prayed, and my prayers were not in vain, for He spared
me until, led by His providence, I heard and understood the truth as taught
in His Holy Word, that the evidence of sins forgiven was in His promise,
and not in our feelings. In other words, we know that when we come to
Him in His own appointed way He will accept of us and forgive all our sins,
because He has promised to do so; and when we do what He requires of us,
we know He will fulfill His promise in our behalf. Our Savior gave Peter
the keys of the kingdom, and one of those keys Peter used on the day of
Pentecost, when, "speaking as the Spirit gave him utterance," he named the
conditions which should open the door of Christ's kingdom to the Jewish
people. When he had preached Christ to them they believed, for we read

that they were pricked in their heart, and cried out unto Peter and the rest of the Apostles, "Men and brethren, what shall we do? Then Peter said unto them, Repent and be baptized, every one of you, in the name of Jesus Christ for the remission of sins, and ye shall receive the gift of the Holy Ghost. For the promise is unto you and to your children and to all that are afar off, even as many as the Lord our God shall call. And with many other words did he testify and exhort, saying, Save yourselves from this untoward generation. Then they that gladly received His word were baptized, and the same day there were added unto them about three thousand souls. And they continued steadfastly in the Apostles' doctrine and fellowship and in breaking of bread and in prayers." This we find recorded in the 2d chapter of Acts, from the first verse to the 42d, inclusive.

The 10th chapter of Acts shows us that Peter was afterwards called upon to use the same key (conditions) which should admit the Gentile world, as up to this date the door of Christ's kingdom had been closed to them. Thus the people spoken of by Peter as "afar off," upon the same conditions which the Jews in the beginning received, were permitted to enter the kingdom of Christ. Reading the above-named chapter carefully leaves no room for doubt concerning this conclusion. And as the Pentecostians and Cornelius gladly received the Word and were baptized, even so did I, rejoicing in the blessed privilege thus given, immediately enter Christ's kingdom, returning to my home with an evidence of sins forgiven which can never be gainsaid, for it rests upon His blessed promise; and from that date to the present, although I have often had occasion to doubt myself, I have never doubted His Holy Word, for the promises are "yea and amen in Christ Jesus our Lord." For over fifty years I have known that He never disappoints those who put their trust in Him. Though our best efforts are imperfect, He graciously looks upon us in the face of His anointed and sees Christ as our righteousness; and thus in His strength we are encouraged to strive on, until, by adding to our faith courage, knowledge, temperance, patience, godliness, brotherly kindness and charity, we may at the last obtain an abundant entrance into the everlasting kingdom of our Lord and Savior, Jesus Christ. Thus, according to Peter—second epistle, from verse and chapter 1st to verse 11th, inclusive—we are shown how the second key opens the everlasting door through added conditions of the Gospel. Our Savior said: "Unto thee will I give the keys of the kingdom of heaven" (Matt. 16:19), and since one key only is required to open one door, we are forced to the conclusion that faith, repentance and baptism unlocked the door of His kingdom on earth, and the additions to our faith, already quoted, unlocked the door which opens to us beyond death's portals. I am so grateful to our Father in heaven that a subject of such vital importance to us has not been left obscure or uncertain, but that the Bible is full of loving, plain but positive, assurance in all that pertains to our salvation, both as to what has been done for us and in what is required of us. I have dwelt upon this event of my life, because out of it has grown my greatest happiness, for "godliness is profitable unto all things having the promise of the life that now is and that which is to come." My happiness was increased by returning from Canada to my childhood's home in New York State, where we remained a few years, living in one of my father's houses; then once more I left my native home, never again to return except to visit, but I was older, more useful and much happier during the years that followed, until another great change came into my life.

The last move to which I have alluded was made to a place called Royal Oak—in Michigan—twelve miles from Detroit. At that time they were laying the first car track from that city to the little town of Royal Oak, the cars to be drawn by horses, and the road for a time to terminate at Royal Oak. As there was other work connected with it, a gentleman who had charge of the industry spoke to my husband about board- ing the hands at work for him. I at first objected, thinking the work- men would probably be a rougher class than I cared to have my children become accustomed to, but he assured us there should be no profanity allowed; so all one winter I cooked for eighteen men without assistance, and baked all my bread in a tin oven and bake kettle. Then Mr. Simonton, considering me competent, solicited us to take the Railroad Exchange, which he owned, and wished us to board himself and family. We took the hotel, and during the time we occupied it occurred the political campaign in which

"Tippecanoe and Tyler, too," was sung and echoed from early dawn to dewy eve, and when they were expected to pass through Royal Oak with their long processions of wagons, log cabins, etc., it occurred to me that they would sing and shout themselves hungry, and that extensive preparations for a dinner would prove agreeable to some of the crowd and profitable to ourselves. But the proprietor's wife, my husband and others discouraged the effort, thinking the crowd would provide themselves with food, which doubtless many of them did, but I, still thinking it best, unaided and without encouragement, prepared a dinner for over sixty people, and at the dinner hour there came such a rush that the only pity was preparation had not been made for a hundred instead. So it was unanimously conceded a good thing that I followed the dictates of my own judgment in the matter. I have mentioned these things particularly that you may understand it was not an idle boast when I said I had grown more competent as well as older, and I am sure you will excuse the seeming appearance of egotism in these reminiscences when you are reminded that I am over eighty-three years old.

"I am old, so old that childhood days seem
   In the shadowy past but a mystical dream;
They are fading away, yet each year of the past
   I love to live o'er, and shall cling to the last
To my few treasured relics, my few withered flowers,
   That tell of the wealth of those sunnier hours.
Oh to live eighty years, eighty long fitful years!
   Yet their smiles and their joys, their griefs and their fears
Are gone as the clouds that are hurrying by
   To dim for a moment the fair summer sky.
I have lived a long life, though it seems a brief day—
   Four score, and God's mercy still brightens my way."

But to resume. After the lapse of a few more years, another change seemed advisable; my husband, who for years had been in feeble health, was visibly failing with great rapidity. Our last move was to Detroit, and

during the remainder of the time that Mr. Balch lived we kept boarders,
and in this way contributed to the support of our family.   Again I was left
a widow, and as nursing the sick offered a better remuneration than anything else I considered myself capable of doing, I decided to engage in it
as a business, and as a homeopathic nurse I took my first lessons of Dr. Ellis,
of Detroit.   I should perhaps earlier in my narrative have mentioned the
names of three of my father's brothers, not that they were all the uncles I
had, but because, although our paths diverged for years, they again met and
crossed, which necessarily connects them with this life story as it proceeds.
There were Uncles John, Elijah and Cyrus K. Anderson, who in my early
home had often constituted a part of our family, and as a matter of course
I was very much attached to them.   Uncle Cyrus, the youngest of all my
father's brothers, was a man of more than ordinary ability and attainments.
While young, he had chosen a collegiate course rather than the "of age pat-
rimony" which his elder brothers had received, and he fortunately obtained
both.   He married a daughter of Judge Clois (a man of some note in the
East), and afterward moved to Buffalo, N. Y., where for several successive
years he filled offices of trust, was County Clerk, Treasurer, etc.   And it
speaks well for his private life that after the death of his first wife, in due
course of time, he married another of the Judge's daughters.   They were
both lovely women, and well do I remember the happy hours spent with
them at our house (their country home) and at theirs (our city home).   But,
in the later years of which I am writing, he had moved to Chicago (the
Garden City of the West, as it was then called), and was living with his
third wife, whose maiden name was Harriet Wilbur, and she, too, was a beautiful woman.   My Uncles John and Elijah, with their wives—women of
blessed memory to me—were also living here, Uncle John having bought a
farm about eight miles from the court house, and Uncles Cyrus and Elijah
occupied a house together in the city.   I have been thus minute in describing, as even their places of residence had a part in shaping this humble life
history.   But I am anticipating.   Uncle Cyrus invited me to spend the
winter with him in Chicago, thinking, I suppose, that it would afford me rest
and recreation and might in other respects prove a benefit.   I accepted his

kind invitation, and, after making arrangements for my older children to remain in Detroit for the winter, I took my two-year old baby boy and turned my face Westward. So in the autumn of 1846 I first looked upon Chicago, then but a babe as compared with its present dimensions, though still a very promising infant, as time has verified. Arriving at my uncle's house with my little boy is but the beginning of new experiences of my life history.

CHAPTER SECOND.

UPON arriving, I was warmly welcomed by my relatives, but after a time I realized that it could not always be convenient to have one visitor who all the time occupied the guest-chamber. And though Uncle Cyrus would have taken the whole house, I would not for a moment allow Uncle Elijah and Aunt Matilda to be thus inconvenienced by moving at that time of the year; so I made it unnecessary by accepting a situation at Dr. Shipman's to wean little Kittie, their first child. (I have since nursed her with two of her own little ones, also her sister Helen with one.) I learned their need of some one through a gentleman who was acquainted with Dr. Shipman, and staying at my uncle's between opportunities for nursing was much more satisfactory to me. And this was the way I first became acquainted with Dr. Shipman and his wife, who at that time were boarding with a private family. But about a week after I went there, they changed to the Tremont House, and I was afterward with them when boarding at the Sherman House, and finally went with them when they moved to the North Side, that being the first they had kept house in the city. After this, I nursed under Dr. Shipman's practice for about seven years, and then I was married to Mr. Dickey, of Amanda, Ohio, and for some years following was absent from Chicago. Of the years spent in Ohio I will not now speak, as I wish, if permitted, in the future to publish that part of my life by itself, as it contains subject matter more than sufficient to fill a book.

After my return to Chicago, I again nursed the sick, under Dr. Shipman's practice principally, so my opportunities for becoming very well acquainted with Dr. and Mrs. Shipman were not limited. And I may be allowed to say right here that I as much believe Dr. Shipman was appointed to carry out this faith work in behalf of the poor little outcasts of this city, as I believe that Moses was " raised up " to lead the children of Israel out of Egyptian captivity; not through miraculous endowment, but by virtue of his birth and education, being, as he was, the son of a very religious and exceptionally benevolent father. Mr. Cleaver, of Cleaverville, told me shortly after Dr. Shipman founded the home that he presumed there was not another man in the city of Chicago who could so entirely command the confidence of the people as did Dr. Shipman. " For," said he, " I know of more than a hundred families that the Doctor, in addition to the medical treatment given, has helped to furnish with necessary supplies to tide them over their time of destitution." And I know that the Doctor with his family always kept what was called " the Lord's bank " in his house, although he had a large family of his own. In looking back to my first winter in Chicago, I am led to recount the mercies of Him who by His hand was then as now leading me, for whenever circumstances seemed to close one door against me my way was being opened in another direction, in manifestations which could not admit of doubt. During the winter, I made arrangements to stay with a family where I could keep my little boy with me, expecting to remain until spring, but a requirement entirely unforeseen aroused my dignity, and I decided to leave. Still I felt troubled, as I respected them very highly. Under these circumstances, imagine my surprise and gratitude when the following morning my Uncle John came to the city for the express purpose of taking me home with him, because while I was grieving, Uncle John dreamed that he pulled me out of the fire, and at four in the morning he said, " Lydia, get me some breakfast, so I can go and get Laura, for she is in trouble." I gladly returned with him, and when, after a time, I again engaged in nursing, Uncle John and Aunt Lydia kept my little boy. So between the rest of mind afforded by the good care given my child and the intervals between work pleasantly spent with all the uncles' families, the winter was soon gone, and with the opening spring my children came. I still continued nursing however, and during those years I took care of Mrs. Shipman twice, also two of William B. Ogden's sisters, Mrs. Sheldon and Mrs. Jones, Mrs. Mahlon Ogden, Mrs. Cleaver and others who are remembered with pleasure. I feel very proud of many now grown into young manhood and womanhood upon whom I bestowed first care in the capacity of nurse. I took care of Mrs. George R. Davis when little Bennie Davis came as a New Year's gift. He is now a promising young man, engaged in studying law. And Bennie Grout, whose life I was permitted to save, will soon graduate as a physician and surgeon, so you will admit that I have good reason to be proud of my Bennies. In reviewing the past, I feel assured that I was made an instrument in the hands of God of doing good to others as well as maintaining myself. I will now give one more incident, as connected with my nursing days, before closing this chapter. I took care of a young man by the name of Charles Clark. He was a member of the Poughkeepsie League, a school where one hundred and twenty men had bound themselves together to care for one another in time of need. Charley's was the first case of sickness, and a serious case it was to them all. Dr. Bebee, the great surgeon, amputated his leg twice, and for a time his life hung in the balance, but after five weeks, at great expense and with the best of care, he recovered sufficiently to be taken home. The league then paid me $50 for my services, and I, knowing what great expense they had incurred, thought the league should be commended for their good work, and wrote—

Men may say what they will do—
Words of loving kindness too
Are very good;
But actual deeds
Done by the league,
Are better understood.
Such deeds must tell—
Must bind Satan in his cell.
To Christ our Lord we give all praise
That men bind Satan in these days.
Hail glorious morn, millennial day,

We shall bind Satan in this way!
All monarchies the earth around,
By men and means they must be bound.
And we will pray
That Christ our Lord hasten the day
That Satan is bound a thousand years
And Christ will dry the nation's tears.
Deeds of kindness, words of love,
Are like dew-drops from above.

Then I inclosed $5, adding—

Most noble league,
My mite I freely give to thee
As my initiating fee,
For as this league is like no other,
I thought, perhaps, it needs a mother.

Mr. Dudley, President of the league, replied as follows:

DEAR MOTHER:—Good woman that thou art, may God ever protect and bless you in your good work. Allow me at this my first opportunity to express to you the heartfelt thanks of each and every member of the E. N. B. C. League for your ever kind and watchful attention manifested in behalf of our dear brother, Charles Clark, during the sad hours of his affliction, and to acknowledge the receipt of $5 liberally donated by you for his relief. God speed you in the right is the wish of your friend as well as son,

A. W. DUDLEY,
President of the E. N. B. C. League,
Chicago, Ill.

And I was also told that the league unanimously accepted my offer of becoming their mother, and so I became the mother of one hundred and twenty sons in a day. Not a common experience, I think you will admit. It was thirty years since this letter was written to the league, and I there expressed the way in which I believed Satan was to be bound, and will add a later expression of my views as given in a letter to my daughter shortly after the Prophetic Convention at Farwell Hall, which I had attended.

THE WOMAN'S VIEWS ABOUT THE RETURN OF THE JEWS AT THE PERIOD WHEN DANIEL'S SAINTS POSSESS THE KINGDOM.

CHICAGO, Nov. 22, 1886.

DEAR JULIA:—I went every day last week to the prophetic meeting to hear about the wonder-working God among the destinies of men and nations, and I must say God has wonderful men to defend His cause. Such harmony of spirit prevailed through the whole session as was pleasant to witness.

Although they differed in thought as to how it was, yet on the question of the second coming of Christ at the millennium they are a unit. They think at Christ's appearing will be a first resurrection and the conversion of the Jews. From what they teach of pre-millennials and post-millennials, I discover that I don't believe like either one of them, all my knowledge being derived from the Bible and a book called " The Vision of the Ages." Every person can read their millennial views in their works, so I have only to state my views.

I believe with these men in the signs of the times, and that we are very near the end of this age of time, and that great events are at the door. I believe in the great tribulation, but I look at it different from their idea. I think, in God's controversy with the nations, His battle will be with the anti-Christ host that wants to take the earth. This will be a literal battle of the wicked one against the Messianic nations. Jesus is represented in the nineteenth chapter of Revelation as being in front of the battle, having on His vesture and on His thigh a name written, King of Kings, and Lord of Lords, and His name is called the Word of God.

The Messianic nations hold up the Word of God to the people; the anti-Christ will do all they can to hide the Word and keep the people in ignorance. Jesus, the Word, is represented in front, and will overcome the wicked host that purposes to possess the earth. Daniel says in the seventh chapter, " And the kingdom and dominion, and the greatness of the king-

dom under the whole heavens, shall be given to the people of the saints of
the Most High." Jesus will not leave the mediatorial throne till He comes
to the judgment. The Jews will gather in Jerusalem, and will tarry till
Jesus comes to the judgment, a Jewish nation. They are one of the witnesses; they witness for the Old Testament—the Christians for the New
Testament. Jesus, the Word, God with us, will rule till the heathen are His
possession, through Daniel's saints; this will harmonize with the Word,
" The first will be last, and the last first;" the Jews, being first, rejected Christ;
the Gentiles accepted Christ, causing them to be first. Daniel's saints, with
the Messianic nations, will rule the Christ-kingdom politically, and Christ
the Lord will be the governor of the earth through His word. At that
period, with the power of the beast and the false prophet destroyed, and
the dragon bound, there is nothing in the way of the Gospel of the kingdom. The laws of the kingdom will protect the Jews in their rights as
Jews. They can receive the Gospel or remain under their own law. God
gives them the gift, as Paul hints, without repentance; but He will not let
them worship idols any more. God says by the mouths of the prophets,
" Ye are my witness." We are the two witnesses, the Jews and the Christians. The " Vision of the Ages " teaches that the nations which believe
in Christ will politically govern the earth.

The Young Men's Christian Association a few years ago had a national
convention in Chicago, the object being to get the name of God in the constitution. Our nation took no notice of the call. One of the speakers said,
" Brethren, we have failed; but I will tell you what is the matter; this was
our time to put the name of God in the constitution; when God's time
comes to have His name in the constitution, it will go in." One woman in
that small assembly of about sixty people in Farwell Hall, said, " Glory to
God!" A gentleman at the close of the meeting grasped her hand and said,
" I want to shake hands with you for responding at such an appropriate
moment." The woman knew then what she knows now, that in the new order
of coming events Jesus would govern the earth through His word, by His
saints, or, in other words, through the Messianic nations. How appropriate
that the Christian Association has their part of the work ready, namely—

to put the name in when God's time comes! We see now why God's name has not been in these human governments.

After the battle of the Almighty God, the Bible nations, with the Word of God as their guide, will rule the whole earth.

When Christ was on earth, the people said to Him that Elias was first to come; and He answered that John was Elias, if they could bear it, meaning that they had a oneness of spirit. The resurrection of the martyrs is spoken of, and they are to live and reign with Christ a thousand years. The " Vision of the Ages " teaches that like spirits with the martyrs will give their life unto death for the liberty of the Gospel.

One thing remember, the Jews don't reject God. They are believers in God. They are very useful to Christians as monumental witnesses. At the time Daniel's saints possess the Kingdom, we have reason to think by the Scriptures that the Jews will be returned to their own land, and their return honors God's promise, and shows the nations that He is a covenant-keeping God. He said He would scatter them, and He said He would return them to their old estates, better than at the beginning. In reading Ezekiel, observe the last verse—the Lord is there. The Lord protects them when the government of the whole earth rests upon His shoulders. The only way left for us to do is to accept it as it reads, and it plainly reads that after the Jews return they worship according to the law in their temple. Read Ezekiel 43rd, 44th and 46th chapters, where the Prince is not allowed to enter the east gate. Read the thirty-fifth chapter and verse where it says, " because thou hast said these two nations and these two countries shall be mine." I understand that these enemies of Christ say these Jews and these Christian dogs shall not possess the earth, but Christ the Word has promised to have dominion over the whole earth, and no one can doubt His protection and deliverance to His two witnesses. Everything said in Ezekiel represents Jewish worship at that period as sanctioned by the Holy Spirit of promise. They have served their full time in being a scattered people, and God will show them, though they reject Him, that He will cause them to be protected by the people that accepted Him; for it is the Christ-people that will have the rule under the whole heavens. Thus they will be pro-

tected in the political government of God down through the thousand
years, and in a body be allowed to govern themselves under the government of Christ; but the saints will have the political reign, and will rule
the earth with a rod of iron, which indicates great power.

Some people have fallen into line to believe that Christ cannot fight
our battles unless He comes in person; but we cannot limit the power of
God. He came to earth to redeem it from bad government, and thus help
man to be free to accept or reject His counsels; and while some say the
earth is growing worse, I claim it is growing better; when we compare the
present with the past, I think we should take courage, as this is the last battle. Although war is a calamity, yet we are no better than other people
who have had to defend the right and forward the cause of Christ by
overcoming the powers that be by the evil one, the enemy to all right
government.

I know that my children will wish me to explain how the dragon is to
be bound a thousand years. Ezekiel says, when this host comes up to battle that only one-sixth part goes back alive. The people that fought for the
dragon will not get what they fought for, the kingdom, but they will be
overthrown, the horse with his rider; so Satan during the thousand years
has no one to fight his battles; he is restrained, or bound in the bottomless
pit, till Christ's bride, the church, finishes the work commenced of covering
the earth with the knowledge of God as the waters cover the sea. Christ
has kept His word; His dominion is an everlasting dominion. God cannot
fail, and all who trust in Him will be at His right hand in the judgment day,
when He comes to be admired of His saints and take vengeance on them
that know not God and obey not His Gospel. O, how beautiful is the plan
of salvation, and all of God's goodness to the whole earth! When He sent
His Son to us the whole earth politically was governed by the evil one, and
Christ died and rose again to establish His kingdom in the hearts of men,
bringing in the new covenant, helping men to redeem the earth from bad
government.

At the end of the thousand years, when all the earth has been redeemed
from the power of Satan through good government, and every people and

nation have been taught the redeeming love of Christ, those who reject the Lord at that period the Lord will reject at His second coming; then is said, " Behold, I come quickly, and my reward is with me; he that is unjust, let him be unjust still; and he that is filthy, let him be filthy still; and he that is righteous, let him be righteous still; and he that is holy, let him be holy still."　　　　　　　　From your Mother,

MRS. LAURA DICKEY.

As the above was written nearly eleven years ago, I will say in conclusion that I am still investigating and receiving added light on this subject. That I believe we are now in the *preparation day*, and that the men and means which our Heavenly Father is employing to bind Satan will be found in the Young Men's Christian Association, in the Temperance reform, in the Labor question, in the Grand Army of the Republic, and in the Christian Endeavor Society, as all these represent a united non-sectarian effort, which will, we believe, eventually merge the government of the people into more direct government of God, thus making the government of God and the government of the people identical. And if Charles A. L. Totten is right in his views concerning the destiny of the lost tribes of Israel, giving Ephraim as England and Manassah as America, then Mrs. Dickey and Prof. Totten have solved the Jewish question.

VIEWS ON THE PROPHECIES.

WHEN Jesus came to His earth, the Prince of the power of the air was holding possession politically, Satan occupied an airy foundation. When Christ came He set up His kingdom in the heart of man, and thus He has leavened all Christendom with Gospel and liberty, and the promise of God is through Abraham that Israel shall inherit the earth. Revelation xix chapter, 10th verse, says: "The testimony of Jesus is the spirit of prophecy."

The 10th chapter of Revelation says: "The ten witnesses testified in sackcloth and ashes for a long time."

Revelation xii chapter, 13th verse: "And when the dragon saw that he was cast unto the earth, he persecuted the woman which brought forth the man-child."

14th verse: "And to the woman were given two wings of a great eagle, that she might fly into the wilderness, into her place, where she is nourished for a time, and times, and half a time, from the face of the serpent."

15th verse: "And the serpent cast out of his mouth water as a flood after the woman, that he might cause her to be carried away of the flood."

16th verse: "And the earth helped the woman; and the earth opened her mouth, and swallowed up the flood which the dragon cast out of his mouth."

Remember, the woman, Christ's Church, represents those that fled into the wilderness—the Puritans. Also remember, Christ gave the emblem, this great eagle, to AMERICA.

Revelation xvii chapter, 15th verse: "And he saith unto me, The waters which thou sawest, where the whore sitteth, are peoples, and multitudes, and nations, and tongues."

This represents the water as peoples, and multitudes, and nations, and tongues, that were and are sent to destroy the woman, Christ's Church. But the earth helped the woman, this great eagle government, and kept the serpent from destroying the woman.

When Christ said to the Disciples, "A little leaven leaveneth the whole lump," thus He leavened His Disciples with Gospel and liberty. Ingersoll and all men that love liberty will fight for this earthly government just as soon as any Christian, for all Christendom was leavened with liberty at the same time that Christ leavened His Disciples with the Gospel.

The Captain of our salvation is a great general, and has put all men, small and great, that love liberty in a way to preserve His earth from the beast and the false prophet. And the dragon will come soon to make war on the woman, and we say, "Lord, come quickly." The army of the Lord is getting ready to fight this last battle, and Christ, through His army, the people, will fight the dragon, and take away his power to fight us any more.

Emperor William says in his speech: "To us the church is not only a memorial of the Reformation, but a serious admonition, and an expression of divine blessing through the Protestant church."

The confession of our faith that we make to-day in the presence of God binds us and the whole of Christendom. Therein lies the bond of peace, reaching beyond all lines of division.

In the matter of faith there is no compulsion. Free conviction of the heart and the decisive acknowledgment thereof is a blessed fruit of the Reformation. We Protestants make feud with nobody on account of the belief, but we hold fast our faith in the Gospel unto death.

The dedication of Martin Luther's church, so long delayed, the Emperor says his father and grandfather longed to see accomplished in their day, and their posterity have succeeded in carrying out their desires. The Emperor has at last fearlessly accomplished their wish. I believe fear of the people kept this dedication from being accomplished long ago. In God's time He has provided the valiant Emperor with courage and power to carry out the wish of his forefathers. To me it looks significant of the signs of the times, as much as to say to the dragon, " Come on, we will fight to the death for our liberty."

Eight years ago I wrote "The Woman's Views About the Return of the Jews." I then said Christ would not leave the mediatorial throne to set up a kingdom, for He had set up His kingdom in the heart of man, and the seventh part of time belongs to Christ and His people, to take a rest in the government of God.

We are nearing the great day when the battle of God, through His people, shall fight the dragon, so Daniel's saints can possess the earth; then the knowledge of God shall cover the earth as the water covers the sea. At that time if a man lives a hundred years and is a sinner, the Lord syas, "Let him be accursed" (means second death). He has been given time to learn which is better, righteousness or sin, bad or good government.

This battle with the dragon will show who controls the earth this time, the Lord or the Devil. According to the Word of God, the dragon will be bound and the people on God's earth will enjoy peace and righteousness in the government of God.

Prof. Totten says : "We are some of the lost tribes of Israel. England is Ephraim and we are Manassah, that went over the walls when our forefathers fled from persecution and came to this wilderness to worship God."

I am thankful that I am privileged to live so near the seventh part of time. If God spares my life to come in and take possession of the inheritance promised to Israel, the whole earth—if I can live to see the government of God and the government of the people identical—I will be thankful. I am thankful now, and can say like old Simeon, "I am ready to depart in peace; not my will but Thine be done."

I said in the "Woman's Views:" "The Jews will remain in a body as Jews through the Millennium, to witness for the Old Testament."

We read of two witnesses, two olive bowls of oil, two olive trees and seven golden candlesticks. We learn that beauty and bands shall be united as one stick.

I will explain how I understand the two witnesses. The Old Testament is one witness, and the New Covenant, called the New Testament, is a witness; the Jews witness with the Old Covenant and the Christians with the New Covenant. Thus we have the need of one olive bowl of oil of prophecy for the Old Covenant and one for the New Covenant.

The two olive trees witness the same; these two witnesses mean two, and remain two in my mind.

I consider the Jews that rejected Christ a monumental witness for the Old Testament, and we need their witness to prove our own position in the New Covenant.

The seven golden candlesticks to the seven churches are to light us through the seventh part of time.

Isaiah lvi, 10th verse, says: "His watchmen are blind; they are all ignorant, they are all dumb dogs, they cannot bark; sleeping, lying down, loving to slumber. Yea, they are greedy dogs which can never have enough, and they are shepherds that cannot understand; they all look to their own way, every one for his gain, from his quarter."

I do hope Isaiah did not mean us; if I could only think that he meant the Jews; but really, I am afraid he meant us, too. As for myself, I have been doing a good deal of barking, and if I have said anything wrong in explanation, or any other way, I will be glad to be told in a common-sense way what it all means.

In the thirty-third of Ezekiel we find the duty of the watchman. No man has set me as a watchman, but I am watching the signs of the times. Over forty years ago I was reading in Daniel, and Daniel said, "The wise should understand." I said, "Daniel, I don't understand a word you say, but I will try." I have kept my promise; I have tried to understand by reading the Bible and other books—"The Messiahship," the great demonstration written by Walter Scott, Standard office, Cincinnati; "The Vision of the Ages," Christian Publishing Company, S. T. Lewis, Manager. Those books in a measure guided me to think and study, and read and run. And now God gives us a man who is writing books called "The Romance of History," and he says we are lost Israel found in ourselves. I am glad to believe we are Israel, because Israel is to inherit the earth. You will notice in reading the Prophets that Judah and Israel are separately mentioned. Jeremiah xxx: 3: "For, lo, the days come, that I will bring again the captivity of my people Israel and Judah, saith the Lord." In the fourth verse, "And these are the words concerning Israel;" twenty-fourth verse, "In the latter days ye shall consider it." If I get the idea right, Israel will rule in the Kingdom of God in the seventh part of time, and Israel will protect Judah in her rights to worship God as she understands; and Judah shall be allowed to choose her own governor from her own people to govern her affairs, but the Jews will be tributary to the government of God through Israel.

The Lord our Righteousness will be King over and through Israel and will rule this time, and Judah accepts Israel's rule and the righteous government of God through Israel. According to promise, Israel shall inherit the earth. I solved the Jewish question five years previous to reading Professor

Totten's book. A Presbyterian minister said: "Mrs. Dickey, if you have solved the Jewish question, you have done more than any man has done." I replied, "I have solved it to my satisfaction." I feel greatly indebted to Professor Totten, for I could not see why Judah and Israel were separately mentioned until I read his works.

I promised to explain the four faces in the first chapter of Ezekiel as I understand them. The face of a man represents Christ. Christ came as a man, and represents all men. Cornelius said to Peter, Acts x: "A man came to him in bright clothing." The face of the lion is England. The face of the ox represents the strength of Germany. The face of the eagle represents America. And when Almighty God fights with the dragon to get control of His own earth, then the four faces, Christ, England, Germany and America, will ally their powers to fight the dragon; and when the dragon gets whipped he is bound. Read Zachariah 3d chapter, 8th verse: "Hear now, O Joshua the high priest, thou and thy fellows that sit before thee; for they are men wondered at; for, behold, I will bring forth my servant the BRANCH." Read 9th and 10th verses and all of Zachariah, and open your eyes for the past and the present, and you will learn the BRANCH, as I understand it, means Israel. We are the temple of God made without hands. I still believe the Jews will build a temple for Jewish worship. The reason I believe this is the way it is written in the 44th and 46th chapters of Ezekiel. I think they will witness in their temple for the Old Testament till Christ comes in person, when Christ will destroy the last enemy, which is death. Christ has come and been coming with spirit and power, helping His people to destroy the beast, the false prophet, and is coming in the same spirit and power to overcome the dragon, and thus He will help His Bride, the Church, to gain the victory and claim with Christ the government of the whole earth in the name of the King of Kings and Lord of Lords. His Bride will occupy till He comes in person. II Peter, 3d chapter, says: "The earth also and the works that are therein shall be burned up." The dragon represents the Devil and he is the last enemy that Christ will destroy, which means death. Death is swallowed up in victory. Thanks be to God, who giveth us the victory through our Lord Jesus Christ! And soon, thank God, we will sing the Song of Victory, of Moses and the Lamb, and the Songs of the Church. The Bride will resound to the ends of the earth; Jesus is the root and offspring of David; the Bright and Morning Star, Christ, will go forth with His nations represented as a man. The dragon that had control of the earth when Christ came to His own and they received Him not is cast down and bound. Christ said, "I come to send the sword," and now with the Church, His Bride, we are promised a rest.

When Eve listened to the serpent, he took possession of her heart. When Christ came, He leavened the heart of man with His Word, His plan, and thus brought good-will to man. When we realize that woman was and is the mother of every man and woman that was and is born, it is a great thought. She was also the mother of the Son of God. We can see that what the woman lost in Adam she gained in Christ. Christ has bestowed great honor on the woman, being the seed of the woman. Through the promise of God the seed of the woman shall bruise the serpent's head. I don't expect the Lord to come in person till the end of the Millennium. I expect He will give us possession of the earth to occupy till He comes. God always has a man when He needs him most, and through a man He has raised up one to let us know who we are. He has written "The Romance of History." God reminds us of His promise that Israel shall inherit the earth. Professor Totten says we are one of the lost tribes of Israel. We have eyes to see and ears to hear; it will be well to read the promises of God and notice the signs of the times, and awake out of sleep, lest trouble come on us unawares. We shall need preparation lest the thief come and find us not ready to go to the Master, and hold fast our faith, come what will. This tribulation that is at the door will then show which of us is on the side of the Lord. O, Lord, help us to be ready with oil in our lamps, to go in unto the marriage of the Lamb. I am aware when we accept Christ in faith we are the true seed of Israel. Paul says: "I have espoused you to one husband, that I may present you as a chaste virgin to Christ." Also there is neither male nor female in Christ Jesus. We are all baptized in the same name. The word of God is spirit and is truth. I believe God's word is His promise and will be kept by His power in spirit and in truth. She truly is a foolish virgin that does not prepare to meet the Bridegroom. We ought to rejoice to know our faith in Christ through His promise to Abraham delivers us from paganism and unbelief. O, woman! be glad and rejoice, for Christ is the friend of woman. The Lord says: "O Israel, thou has destroyed thyself, but in me is thine help. I will be thy king; where is any other that may save thee in all thy cities?" (Hosea xiii, 9.) Zachariah xii, 5: "And the governors of Judah shall say in their hearts, The inhabitants of Jerusalem shall be my strength in the Lord of Hosts their God." Seventh verse: "The Lord also shall save the tents of Judah first, that the glory of the house of David and the glory of the inhabitants of Jerusalem do not magnify themselves against Judah."

Read all of the ninth chapter of Zachariah. The thirteenth verse says : "When I have bent Judah for me, filled the bow with Ephraim, and raised up thy sons, O Zion, against thy sons, O Greece, and made thee as the sword of a mighty man." Sixteenth verse: "And the Lord their God shall save them in that day as the flock of his people." It would be well if all the people would read the Word of God, and, as Paul said to Timothy, learn to divide the Word of truth in order for instruction to ourselves and others.

The twelfth chapter of Revelation says the dragon made war on the woman. We are looking for him, so Christ's prepared people can bind him and despoil him of his power. When he is bound, we look for a rest in the long-looked-for period in the government of God through His people, the government of God and the government of Israel to inherit the earth according to promise. The government of God in the new order of things will explain why we still pray "Thy kingdom come, Thy will be done on earth as it is in Heaven." There will be no more monarchial governments, such as we now have. Christ will be King of Kings and Lord of Lords; and Daniel's saints through Christ shall rule the earth with a rod of iron. The revenue in the government of God won't be whiskey revenue, it will be peace and righteousness through our amended laws. Jesus promises His people a rest when the beast and false prophets are destroyed and the dragon bound. Glory to God in the Highest, peace on earth and good will to man !

NOTICE.

One thing I feel sure of: When Christ and His Bride take control of the earth, Israel and Judah will be joined into one stick in fight. The covenant was broken between Beauty and Bands and they were cut asunder; but they will be bound together in brotherhood when they fight the Bear.

Israel bears testimony with Christ in the New Covenant. The Jews will continue to bear testimony under the Old Covenant.

NEW COVENANT, KINGDOM OF CHRIST ON EARTH.

THE APOSTLES AND THIRD PERSON IN THE TRINITY.

FOR forty years I have been interested in the Prophecies, and have given much thought to the coming of our Lord, and the means used through the Prophets and Apostles. When Christ came in His ministry He spoke to all the people, and did many miracles manifesting the power of God, and chose the Apostles to be His witnesses, so the new covenant could be written. Jeremiah (xxxi: 31) speaks of a new covenant; also Hebrews, viii: 8. In the seventeenth chapter of St. John, in order to get the meaning of Christ, we should see who He is talking to, and see His purpose in teaching them by His word; and His power that He does all these things in their presence, to prepare them to be His witnesses. In order to understand we should read the book of testimony in St. John, and all the testimonies in the four Evangelists. Then the power of God, manifested through Christ, is seen to prepare His witnesses. Then we perceive Christ's purpose, when, in John xvii: 9, 10, "I pray for them; I pray not for the world, but for them which thou hast given me; for they are thine, and all mine are thine, and thine are mine, and I am glorified in them." Eleventh verse: "Holy Father, keep through thine own name those whom thou hast given me, that they may be one, as we are." In the twenty-second verse Christ prays for His chosen witnesses that they be one "even as we are one." This oneness of spirit is manifested as one man. Twentieth verse, same chapter: " Neither pray I for these alone, but for them also which shall believe on me through *their* word." This proves the object of calling them to witness through Christ, so through them the new covenant could be written, and the words of eternal life could be brought to the world through the Apostles. The third person in the Trinity was endued with power from on high—messengers of the covenant of God to all the world. St. Paul's argument in the eighth chapter of Hebrews puts all in order. No testament can be made till after the death of the testator, and the witnesses to the covenant were necessary to be one in spirit to witness what they had seen and heard. Everything written is witnessed, so the world may receive Christ in His new covenant laws and commands, and believe His promises. This leads us to see the laws of the Kingdom of God. If you will read the four Evangelists with a view to understanding the laws of the new covenant of the Kingdom of God you will find after Christ is risen from the dead (in the last chapter of Mark) His commission to the Apostles was to go and preach the Gospel to every creature. And His promise is: " He that believeth and is baptized shall be saved." And they went and preached everywhere, the Lord working with them and confirming the Word with signs following.

This leads us to see what the miracles were for—to confirm the Word. Then in Matthew xvi, when Christ gave the keys of the Kingdom of Heaven to Peter and said: "Whatsoever thou shalt bind on earth shall be bound in Heaven." Then if you have read the four Evangelists you have learned that Christ told His Disciples to tarry at Jerusalem till they were endued with power from on high. Jesus was translated ten days when Pentecost was fully come. When the Disciples were assembled they were all of one accord in one place (Acts ii chapter). Peter has the keys, and standing up with them (11-14 verses) said: "Hearken to my words." We want to see what Peter binds on earth, as he has the keys of the Kingdom of Heaven. In the thirty-second verse he says: "This Jesus hath God raised up, whereof we all are witnesses." In the thirty-eighth verse Peter preached the law of the

Kingdom of Heaven, and in the fortieth verse he exhorted them to save themselves, showing it was an act they could all do to repent of their sins, and be baptized in the name of Jesus Christ for the remission of sins, and so receive the gift of the Holy Ghost. This corresponds with Christ's words: "As many as receive me I will give power to become sons of God." This power is promised us after we receive Him; sometimes it is called the Comforter, the Holy Spirit. I feel sure it is a comfort to believe in the promises of God, for Jesus Christ is God with us. "In the beginning was the Word, and the Word was with God, and the Word was God, and was made flesh, and dwelt among us, and we beheld his glory, the glory of the only begotten Son of God." It is the Comforter in our souls to know we believe the promises of God, that we are born of God's word of promise. This leads us to inquire how we know. Because Christ said: "Go teach all nations, baptizing in my name."

This brings us to ask how can we get the new name in the new covenant. Peter said, "He baptized in the name of Jesus Christ for the remission of sins and you shall receive the Holy Ghost." We suppose from what Christ said it is power we receive from God. Christ said as many as received Him He would give them power to become sons of God. God placed it in our own power to receive Him. Peter said, "Save yourselves from this untoward generation." God had a plan to bring His word to man. The Father, Son and the Apostles are one in action and in spirit. Thus the three are one, and the person of the oneness of the Spirit is to bear witness of the power of God given to His Son; so that when we receive God's Son we receive power from on high to do the will of God. Faith comes by hearing, and the words of eternal life are inviting us back to a loving Father, and God gives the Apostle the witness of the spirit of power to write the new covenant in order for us to understand when we come into Christ's kingdom on earth we covenant with Christ by coming in His name. I think we have some of the language of Ashdod by calling the Holy Spirit the third person in the Trinity; it blinds the minds of the people to speak of the Spirit in that way. Christ Himself is the personal power of God in the spirit of truth. He is the person, and the Apostles witness with

Him, and according to our finite understanding we could easily see the Apostles were the third person. But again we see the three compose one body and one spirit, and unite all in one power, one spirit, one faith, one Lord, one baptism, one body, fitly joined together in the unity of the spirit of faith in Christ Jesus our God.

This leads to the thought that God will not hear us if we hold iniquity in our hearts. Since we have been forgiven, the loving spirit of forgiveness should abide in us; and if we are born of the spirit of truth, the effect on us will be that we wish everyone would look to Christ and live; for out of Christ there is no eternal life. One thing we ought to remember: When Christ was baptized, God acknowledged Him His Son; and when we are baptized Christ acknowledges us, and gives His promise of the Holy Spirit of power, the Comforter, as long as we abide in the laws of the Kingdom of Heaven. He promises to abide in us if we keep His commandments. He promises eternal life, and is gracious to forgive when He sees we trust in Him and not in ourselves. It is necessary while we live in this world that we should be law-abiding citizens. And when we enter the Kingdom of Heaven in the name of Christ on earth, in order to know the law of Christ we should study His word in prayer and supplication, that the words of Christ be the man of our counsel; and try to be taught of God, for Jesus said to the multitudes that followed Him: "You cannot come to me except my Father that sent me draw you, for all that he drawest are taught of God; and I will raise him up at the last day." This teaches us these men were not taught of God; they were taught doctrines and commandments of men, and cannot be saved, because Christ comes to save men that are drawn by the spirit of the teaching of God. When we obey the laws of the Kingdom of Heaven, the Kingdom is within us, and we shall be able to give a reason for the hope that is within us when we cast our hopes on the promises of God, and not on our feelings as evidence.

Our feelings are evidence to us that the Word of God is truth. These promises of God are so adapted to our wants that we feel this is just what we need; and here Abraham's faith comes good. If we have faith enough to believe in Christ's plan, His Kingdom of Heaven on earth we enter, freed from sin. We have been buried with Christ to represent His death; when we rise from the watery grave we represent our faith in the resurrection of Christ; and as Christ was raised from the grave, so we shall be raised to walk in newness of life if we continue in the Apostles' doctrine of the Kingdom of Heaven on earth. Christ has only left on record two ordinances: one is the order of baptism; the other is the communion with Christ every first day of the week; that reminds us of His broken body and shed blood, and gives us an opportunity to renew our covenant and go forth with the armor of God shielding us from business temptations in the world, knowing the Lord we have trusted in has all power in heaven and in earth, and can supply all our needs according to His promises. The responsibility rests with ourselves to believe Christ's words and go forth observing the laws of the Kingdom of Heaven.

Peter rehearses the laws of the Kingdom of Heaven on earth: "Add to your faith virtue, knowledge, temperance, courage, patience, godliness, brotherly kindness, charity; if these things be in you and abound, you will have an abundant entrance into the everlasting kingdom; and if we lack these things we are blind, and cannot see afar off." After the loving Father has taken us back, through such cost, it becomes our duty to love His advice, and cast ourselves on His mercy, and be thankful to comply with His wish, and cling to the new name and the promises, and work out our salvation with fear and trembling. Not that fear that doubts Christ's word, but the same fear that Paul had, to keep our body under lest we be cast away. Watch and pray lest we enter into temptation; pray without ceasing, which means an unceasing desire to do right.

Our own mistakes let them come as they will, we suffer for them.

We all have the Word of God to guide us unto all truth.

As a man thinketh so is he; it stands us in hand to think right, in order to act right, and rest ourselves on a sure foundation.

It is a great comfort to settle our minds on Christ, a sure resting-place.

If all of us should live according to the advice in the Epistles, we would be living Epistles, known and read of all men; then the world could take knowledge through us and learn of Christ. Paul says, if our

Gospel is hid, it is hid to them that are lost, in whom the god of this world
blinded the minds of them that believe not. Jesus says: "It is the Spirit that
quickeneth the words that I speak unto you; they are Spirit and they are
life." We can find many places where Christ's words are His sure promises;
and we can obey His words if we will; or we can resist the will of God if we
choose; but the responsibility rests with ourselves for disobedience to God.
When Jesus had spoken many went away. Then said Jesus unto the twelve,
"Will ye also go away?" Peter said: "Lord, where shall we go? Thou
hast the words of eternal life, and we are sure that thou art that Christ, the
Son of the Living God."

Jesus gives the reason why all left but twelve. Christ said, "They seek
honor from one another; they love the honor of the world."

I have told you faithfully of the Apostles' doctrine, the visible church
of Christ on earth. And the Apostles have been faithful in describing the
character of the children of the King in all their Epistles, and their advice is
alarming, lest when we have run the race set before us we should lose the
crown of eternal life. In all the Evangelists, Matthew, Mark, Luke and
John, and also in John the Baptist, you will learn that the Kingdom of
Heaven is at hand. It comes without perception; it is within us; and we
are notified by Christ's word that the Kingdom of Heaven is near us.

The reason I have said the Apostles were the third person in the Trinity is because Jesus prayed that they be made one with Him and His Father.
And the Apostle John's testimony (First Epistle, v: 7): "For there are three
that bear record in heaven: the Father, the Word, and the Holy Ghost;
and these three agree in one." The question is, Who are these three that
bear record in heaven?

The Apostles bore record about Jesus Christ's word, and were one
with the Father and the Son, bearing record of Christ's work on earth.
And we also find in Revelation, xxi: 12, 13 verses, that the twelve tribes
of Israel had their names written on the gates, and the Apostles' names were
in the twelve foundations of the lamb. We see from this that the Apostles
represent setting up the Kingdom of Heaven on earth, and their testimony
is the knowledge of Christ to us. When we receive Christ we receive Him

on the testimony of the Apostles, and from their testimony we believe in Jesus Christ. I believe the person represented is the Apostles, and they are the proof to us of Christ's word of truth, and Christ is represented as the truth, and Christ's words are life to the world, for the Apostles have seen Him and His works, and they testify to the power of God through Christ to all men. If you believe in His name and obey His commands you will enter the Kingdom of Heaven on earth, according to His plan, and be made free from sin, and abide in Christ according to the laws of the Kingdom of Heaven. The Apostles' witness is we shall have an abundant entrance into the everlasting kingdom by obedience to the law of the Lord.

I here recognize the person of the Apostles, bringing to us the personality of Christ and the power of Christ to save man by the Divine power of God. I have done the best I can for the children of men, so the Holy Spirit, the power of God, need not rest in obscurity. And man can know when he is born in the name of Christ. When we are born in Christ's name and promises we can know of His Love, for He gave His life for us and became our Passover. When He instituted the Communion in His name and represented it as His broken body and shed blood, then He was ready to give His life for all men. Whomsoever will may come into the Gospel Kingdom on earth. It was the Jewish Passover time when they put Christ to death, and after His resurrection He appeared to His Apostles and other of His brethren forty days, and said to His Disciples, "Tarry at Jerusalem till you are endued with power from on high;" and at the Pentecost time, ten days after Christ ascended, you will find the power of God manifested (in the second chapter of Acts); and Peter opened the door of salvation to the Jews, first in the Kingdom of Heaven on earth in the name of Christ, when they entered according to direction, and had their sins forgiven. After a time, when Christ was ready to receive the Gentiles, God manifested His power, and the Holy Spirit fell on them. Peter speaks of it as a gift that falls on us. At the beginning it was the preparing power of God making known to them that He was ready to take them into His Kingdom of Heaven on earth on condition of obedience—of entrance in the name of Christ. The Christian Jews did not expect that the Gentiles would be allowed to come in, and took Peter to task for admitting them.   Peter says, "What was I that I could withstand God?   I was sent to tell them words whereby they could be saved." So we see God prepares the way to help us to come, but we all have to enter in the name, the same as at the beginning.   When Peter preached to the Jews that had put the just one to death they had to accept the name they had rejected.

If men in our day can take the risk of changing the law of the Lord by taking a promise and misplacing it to suit the doctrines and commandments of men, and make the laws of God of no effect, they can see the effect of their doings now in this unbelieving world and the different names of the Protestant churches.   We deserve the scoffs of the Catholics; they claim one name, one church.   If we had proved true to the Apostles' doctrine, we should have had one name, one church, one Lord, one faith, and one baptism.

The Apostle St. Paul said if any man preached any other doctrine than he preached, let him be accursed; and the curse of all these doctrines of men is upon us in all this Babylon of beliefs; the seed of unbelief is sown, and our nation of unbelief will pay the price, for our cup of iniquity is nearly full; and the people are seeking glory and honor from the world and each other. These men that are teaching the doctrines and commandments of men would not dare teach the laws of the Kingdom of God; the different organizations would scorn a preacher that would not teach the traditions of their church. We are in the toils of Satan, and soon, very soon, and even now, we are passing through tribulation; but this is a bare beginning of the chastisement of God, letting our own individual and national sins punish us.

We all know the name of Christ, and the Scriptures teach His followers were first called Christians at Antioch.   We have counted ourselves unworthy to wear the name of Christ, and the world has its wisdom and counts the wisdom of God and His plan of no account; and the evil one and his sore judgments will be hard to bear.   It was the evil one that changed the law of God so he could rule the earth himself; and the same cause that deceived the world will humble it till he will drive us all together.   God will not hinder the man of sin till he drives us as one man home to the kingdom of Christ on earth.

We have three opposing parties represented: the beast, the false prophet and the dragon. When they are removed the thousand years of peace in Christ's kingdom on earth will come; the temporal power of the beast is gone. That is the reason His personal power is assuming so much power. God said the beast and false prophet should go down together. We have reason to think by the signs of the times they will go into oblivion at the end of this age. It looks now as if we are near the last battle to see who will govern the earth. The zeal of the Lord of Hosts will accomplish this through His people.

The Lord will rejoice when His people, through the power of God, overcome the enemy of God and man; then the dragon will be bound. The same man of sin that changed the laws of God is at our door to send us back to our Father's home in Jesus' name. When that time comes Christ's Bride will rule the whole earth. In the name of Christ, our Lord, we have got to pass through tribulation with this man of sin. When we are driven together in the one name, the Young Men's Christian Association will put the name of Christ, King of Kings and Lord of Hosts, on their banners. They are holding the name for that purpose. Nine years ago this winter they met in Farwell Hall to put the name of God in our worldly constitution. God hindered them. One man gave the reason why they were hindered. He said: "Brethren, this is our time to put the name of God in the constitution; but when God's time comes for His name to go in, it will go in." I said: "Glory to God!" I knew then what I know now. We are nearing the seventh part of time, when Christ's Bride, the church, the Israel of God, will inherit the earth one thousand years. And when we enter in His name we will occupy till He comes in person.

David said the name of the Lord should resound to the ends of the earth. The rule of Christ through His people is described as being as strong as iron. When the man of sin wrested the keys of the kingdom from Peter, he failed to see Peter had a wife, or perhaps in his highness he assumed the name of God to rule the earth, and thought it was not best for God to marry.

If he built his church on Peter, and failed to notice Peter had a wife, and undertook to rule in Peter's name, or in Christ's name, changing the laws of God for greatness and honor, he would be sure to fail, for Christ has and will prevail.

"Glory to God in the highest, peace on earth and good will to man!"

CHAPTER THIRD.

AFTER a few years' absence, I returned to Chicago and resumed nursing, as before stated, and often heard Dr. Shipman speak about the necessity of a Foundlings' Home being established in this city, more especially during the two years immediately preceding the opening of the home on Green Street. It is not necessary for me to repeat why Dr. Shipman was so exercised on this subject; doubtless you are all familiar with his reasons as given by himself. But I do know that it was a matter of conscience with him. He fully realized that it was a great undertaking; yet its magnitude did not deter him from engaging in this much-needed work. When speaking with him about it, previous to its commencement, I told him if he had held a baby over his shoulder as many nights as I had, I did not believe he would care to start a baby home. But, although I did not talk encouragingly, I thought my long experience in the care of babies rendered me capable of giving valuable assistance in that department. Mrs. Fuller, of Lake Avenue, and many others who felt sure that I, through the mercy of God, had been permitted to snatch their babies from the jaws of death, could testify to my efficiency in the care of little ones; so I promised the Doctor, if he entered upon the work, I would give six months in labor; and although circumstances did not favor the exact carrying out of my intentions, what I could not do in one way I endeavored to do in another. As will be shown hereafter, the Doctor would not be discouraged, for his convictions were strong and his faith was equally strong; so he persevered, I need not say with what results, for they are well known to you all. And we need not marvel when we remember that our Heavenly Father possesses the same power to-day that He did when the Children of Israel were enabled to escape from their pursuers by passing through the midst of the sea on dry land; the same power that closed the lions' mouths; that protected His servants in the midst of the fiery furnace, and sent a raven to feed the prophet Elijah. When we think of all God's wonderful manifestations of power through the ages, the only marvel is that we should ever doubt. And evidently Dr. Shipman did not indulge in fears, but practically went to work, and as the first thing to be done was to get a house, Mrs. Shipman and I began assisting him by looking for one. But as she, unfortunately, received a fall which disabled her for walking, I continued alone until the Green Street house was found, and the Doctor thought it would do for a beginning. Our first was a baby boarder, received Monday, January 29, 1871. Tuesday a boy baby was given, and I called him a captain, because he yelled so loud and was so unlike our gentle lady boarder; so the Doctor named him John Captain. Wednesday evening a girl baby was brought, and I asked the Doctor to call her Mary Ann Dickey. I still have her little belt with the name marked on it. The same evening (Wednesday) a poor little sick baby was left. The first item furnished by a reporter was: "A large two-bushel basket to take the babies in; and an old stove," and two ladies who came from the North Side asked: "Why was not the home furnished before being opened?" I replied: "When the babies come, we expect the Lord will send us what we need." And surely our trust was not in vain, for the same evening our sick baby came two men brought a mattress bed, simply saying, "From a friend to the babies," and only the Lord and ourselves knew what a blessing it was. And again, after ten o'clock the same night, the Lord sent us other much-needed supplies, eighteen nice clean baby napkins. The girl who brought them said the lady had just finished them and thought, though late, she would send them, as we might be in need of them. I do not now remember the lady's name, but I know the Lord guided her hand that night. And so the work was going on. Friday a colored baby was brought, making five in less than a week. Saturday I went to Mr. Bangs and bought a stove for twenty dollars, which was delivered the following Monday. I did not intend the Doctor should know that I owned the stove, but he questioned me so closely that I had to tell him. He refused to accept it, saying I could not afford to give it, and beside a larger one would soon be needed, but it could be used a while. I have alluded to the stove that you might better understand some little incidents that afterwards occurred, which will be mentioned later. Now, ladies, I will give you a description of our home family and surroundings at that time. There were five babies, as already stated. An elderly woman by the name of Blodget brought recommendations to Dr. Shipman, and he sent her to the home to assist, and she also had a few dishes and things which she brought along with her. I had happened to meet her once previous to seeing her at the home. When I was introduced to her, she told me that she had been engaged during the war in doing hospital work, and that when they had nice warm soups they tantalized the Confederate soldiers by putting the soup under their noses, then taking it away, and finally giving them the cold slops that were left. I said I also had for a few months done the same kind of service, but that I had treated the poor sick boys alike. She then said: " I know just what you are if that was the way you did; you are a Southern Secesh Copperhead." I answered: " Madam, you do not know me at all; I am a woman who sympathizes with suffering wherever I find it, be it North or South." Of course Dr. Shipman knew nothing about her except through her references, which he had considered satisfactory. Another woman was also sent to help take care of the babies; but oh what helpers they were! The difficulty of obtaining efficient help was one of the many trials of those earlier days—one which no doubt the Doctor realized as a whole, but if he had been subjected to the minutiæ of it, his perplexities, I am sure, would have been greatly increased. The last-named woman, who came into the home as a helper was unkind to the babies; not even the little sick one was excepted. She said if I expected those babies treated as though they were our own, I'd find myself mistaken. I said: " I see I shall, but as far as possible I shall treat them as though they were my own." When the first calling day was announced by the Doctor, I asked the women if they would assist me to wash the babies' clothes, that the little ones might be clean. They said, no, they would not; so I washed them without help, which took all night, as I had to attend to the babies beside. I shall never forget that night's washing and ironing. In the morning I said: "Will you heat a kettle of water to thaw the ice off the steps before anyone attempts to come up them?" Again they refused, saying: "If the Doctor wants it done, let him send someone to do it; " so I attended to it myself; but I felt my strength giving way, and the Doctor told me I would have to go somewhere and get rested. As I had engaged to nurse Mrs. Peck (before knowing when the Doctor would open the home) and the time was drawing near, I went, but was unable to stay with her, and after a few days was taken to my son, near Ottawa, where I was very sick a few weeks. Before I returned to the city, the following May, the home had moved to Randolph Street. They had procured a matron, and also had a maiden lady who dressed the babies, but the poor little things looked as though they had the spotted fever, and Dr. Shipman wanted me to see what I thought about them, for he knew I understood a good deal about babies, and truly it did not take me long to find out what the trouble was, for the bands were brought up close under the arms and fastened so tightly as to impede circulation. This was done so as to make a long body to pin the napkin on, that the flannels might not be in danger of getting soiled, and when I rectified their manner of dressing by putting the bands where they should be worn, and pinning them properly so the poor little things could breathe naturally, they began to recover. I told them, and here repeat, that babies should be dressed from the shoulders if one desires to make them comfortable and healthy. The woman who dressed the babies used to hold up the most pitiable, emaciated one among them and say: "Ain't it an honor to this homeopathic institution?" and the matron sanctioned this impression given against homeopathy. But when it was so plainly seen that it was their own management, or rather mismanagement, that had caused the trouble, they were not at all pleased; and as they had no other redress, they influenced the washerwoman to make things disagreeable for me, because, under the new order of dressing flannels were occasionally soiled. I was not paying strict attention to the washerwoman's tirade, so the matron evidently thought they were failing in their purpose and said: " Mrs. Dickey, that means you." Well! to tell it in a few words, just then I guess they did not think me quite as meek as Moses was said to have been; and as I would not tell the Doctor or Mrs. Shipman of their doings, because I knew they had enough to contend with, I never knew what their misrepresentations were. But the Doctor asked me if I was willing to go to his house with the babies that needed my attention, and as it was much more difficult to take care of them at his house than at the home, there could be but one conclusion. When I went to the home to take care of the sick babies, Mrs. Shipman had told me that as soon as they could have the rear rooms, which were not at first vacated, they had thought it would be a good arrangement to fit them up as a nursery for sick babies and give me charge of them; and I hoped in that way, if I could stand the work, to redeem my promise of six months' labor made to the Doctor. But evidently something had changed their plans, since the Doctor asked me, as before stated, if I was willing to take the babies to his house and care for them. Previous to my going to Dr. Shipman's house, Dr. Ballard, who was at that time assistant physician at the home, said: "I feel better when the babies are better; don't you, Mrs. Dickey?" I said: "No, sir; I always feel worse when the babies are better;" and he laughed, for he understood the hard night and day work that resulted in their improvement, and when I told the Doctor that their manner of dressing was what had caused the babies to look so spotted, he said he had suspected as much. When I first returned to the home, I had been very much gratified to find a matron in charge who seemed so well adapted to the position. She did not profess to know much about babies, but in the domestic department seemed careful and competent. One little incident I will mention which shows her carefulness: At the time I bought the stove of which I have spoken, I also bought a small porcelain kettle, expressly to be used in preparing the babies' food, and while I was caring for the sick babies she refused to let me use it, saying she did not want it "all stuck up." I did not tell her it was my own kettle, but asked her if she then would let me take a basin to prepare the food in. Later, when I was working outside in the interest of the home (as will hereafter be explained), having made arrangements for the furnishing of two rooms, Mrs. Shipman asked the men who were at work in them what day they would be through, and they said she could have the rooms Thursday. Accordingly, the furnishing goods were delivered at that time, but the matron refused to have them brought inside, because the rooms were not entirely completed, so the things were deposited in the yard. But I was afraid they might get wet or something happen to them, and Miss Martin, the linen woman, said: " Mrs. Dickey, I will help you carry them in and find corners for them until they can have their proper places; " then added: " Mrs. Dickey, I should think you would hate the matron for the way she has treated you," and I laughingly replied: " Oh, no; I ought to like her for taking such good care of my little kettle." Again, when the matron was complaining about the inefficiency of the stove, saying it was not large enough, and the oven was cracked and would not bake, I replied that I too would be glad when the new stove came, as then I could take mine away. " Your stove! Your stove! " she exclaimed, " How came it yours? " " Because I bought and paid for it," said I. Still she seemed to discredit my statement, and afterwards said to me:" Mrs. Dickey, now tell me, is this stove really yours, or did Dr. Shipman give it to you for service rendered? " I then answered with emphasis: " I have told you I bought the stove of Mr. Bangs, and if you don't believe me, you can go and ask him if you choose to." I presume it then dawned upon her that she had refused me the use of my own kettle. Shortly after I became acquainted with her, she told me that Dr. Shipman would have to give the home up to the state, for he could not carry it, and it troubled me until I committed it to the Lord in prayer, saying: " Oh Lord, if it is Thy will that Dr. Shipman may succeed in his home work, then it is mine; but if it is not Thy will, neither is it mine," after which I slept in peace. And when she made the same assertion to others, by whom it was repeated, I only thought she expressed her fears, as I had done when he first engaged in this great undertaking. I had often thought, If the Doctor fails in this work, will it leave his beautiful faith and trust unimpaired? One day I said something of this kind to Mrs. Shipman, and she admitted that I had spoken what her own thoughts had sometimes been. And so, when the matron from time to time expressed her conviction of the Doctor's inability to carry on the work, I, of course, supposed that her remarks were prompted by anxiety, but as I afterward learned, through some motive, supposably of a selfish character, it was her intention that he should be hindered from going on with his appointed work, as it was made known that she at different times had told people not to leave money to the home, as it only encouraged the Doctor in making an effort to continue the home work. But time has proven in many ways that it only requires God and one faith worker to constitute a host, and opposition counts as nothing when arrayed against that of which He approves; and when, months after, they had given her an opportunity to resign, and I was informed that it was because she was untruthful and unreliable in many ways, I only said I could have told all that when I was in the home. She told me if she had control she would give the babies paregoric, and I detected some cases where she had sanctioned its use to an alarming extent. I not only knew myself that her word was not to be depended upon, but she had given all in the house plenty of reason to understand the same fact. I had been very careful not to speak an unkind word to her, even under provocation, and I would not speak against her to the Doctor or Mrs. Shipman, knowing how difficult it was to get such helpers as the situation demanded, and, said I, "I knew you would soon enough see for yourselves what she was capable of doing." And they were glad I had not spoken, for to have understood a little then would have complicated the difficulty. I have not thus recounted the matron's shortcomings because I consider it pleasant to recall a person's defects, but rather to impress upon my readers one of the great trials of those early home days. But Dr. Shipman stood the test, and the Lord has rewarded him by supplying—these many years—a corps of amiable, reliable and competent co-workers. First was the Ladies' Aid Society, and through it untold good has been accomplished. When Dr. Shipman's health failed, and it was deemed advisable that he should go abroad, how marvelous it seemed that in such a time of great need Dr. Prince should come, as though sent from the skies; also Mrs. Fox as matron, and Miss Peck, her daughter, who acceptably and efficiently fills the position of matron since Mrs. Fox has grown aged and infirm. I would speak of Mrs. Meserole, Mrs. Trumbo, Mrs. Reed and others as assistants; Dr. Harriet Howe as physician, and Mrs. Brown as housekeeper. In fact, every department is represented by faithful, energetic helpers in this beautiful faith work. And the home building, with all its conveniences and systematic appointments, is in itself a monument of God's mercy to one who has trusted Him implicitly. After what I have written, I think, ladies, you will easily understand why I felt sure that I had been misrepresented to Dr. Shipman when he asked me to go to his house with the babies. I went, but taking care of them there was more exhausting than at the home, more going up and down stairs, and in some other ways less convenient; and the result was I soon had to discontinue the care of the babies; and as this was my second attempt (and failure too), I decided that I should have to try in some other way to redeem my promise to the Doctor. Now, it is well known that no person living in the home has a right to solicit for it, as it is purely a faith institution. But it is equally well understood that the Lord works through means, that His people are His agents. So, having severed my connection with the home, I assumed the responsibility of placing some of its needs before those who were willing to work for the Lord. I first went to Mrs. Potter Palmer, who at that time was an influential member of the Christian Church. She gave ten dollars, and the united efforts of the church ladies furnished two rooms nicely. I next saw Mrs. Elkins, who was spoken of as being very active in every benevolent enterprise. She being a member of the Unitarian Church, the ladies of that church gave seventy-five dollars in furnishing one large room. It will be remembered that the home was still on Randolph Street. Next I went to Mrs. Cleaver, of Cleaverville, to see about getting a stove, and she raised sixty dollars with which to purchase one. I will mention one incident connected with those soliciting days which may interest you. One lady introduced me to her husband, saying: "I want to tell you what he says—'that you are another old fraud, trying to fill your own pocket with money.'" I could not refrain from smiling, but said: "I don't know as

I blame you for thinking so, considering all that is going on these days; but this time you are mistaken, for I do not receive any money, but could show you a pair of blistered feet for my portion." He replied: "I can readily believe they are blistered if you are walking these hot sidewalks; but why do you not take some of the money to ride on?" "Because," said I, "as already stated, I do not receive anything myself, but I have made arrangements that everything given shall be left with Mrs. Stephens, an aristocratic lady living on Michigan Avenue; but I have ten dollars that I have worked and earned, and I am walking to save it, for as long as I can make it last I intend to continue this work for the home; and although I am a poor woman who has to walk, and your wife can ride in her carriage, we are on an equality in this work, and I do not believe if she collected any money that she would keep it." Said he: "Neither do I believe you would." I then replied: "I am in a good deal of a hurry, but intended to stay until you admitted this much." But, though often footsore and weary, an occasional word of appreciation renewed my courage. During those soliciting days, on the 22d of June, I went to the Presbyterian Church social, which was given with a sincere desire to benefit the home, and while there Mrs. Ambrose said: "Mrs. Dickey, I am glad to see you here, for you are the only woman ever in the home who was worth a row of pins." In this way I labored until I felt that I had made my promise good for six months' service. After the new home was built, or rather was in process of building, the Ladies' Aid Society had cards with a cut of the building on them. They were called bricks, and sold for ten cents each. I was offered a percentage for selling them, but chose not to receive it, and so carried seventy dollars from their sale to the home. I am thankful that the Lord has seen fit to use me in this grand faith work. For He knew that my trust was in Him, although I am forced to admit that my standard of faith was far below that of Dr. Shipman's in regard to establishing the Foundlings' Home, and this admission reminds me of the time when Dr. Shipman introduced me to Mrs. Sampson, jestingly, as one of the founders of the home. Said I: "Dr. Shipman, how can so good a man as you make such an assertion, for I am sure the poor babies would have died in the street if founding the home had depended on me; but," addressing Mrs. Sampson, " I will tell you who I am—I am that old woman on whose back the Doctor opened his home and like to broke it." " Yes," said the Doctor, " Mrs. Dickey was like another woman who could not stand it here, only more so." Again, after the great Chicago fire, I told Dr. Shipman he would surely have to give up the home now, for the city was burned, and he replied: " God is just as rich as He ever was." The undiminished prosperity of the home since that period is in itself a lesson to all professing Christians whose faith is weak and uncertain. I scarcely know where to stop when writing on this subject, but as I wish to add some selections and would not weary you, with a few added remarks I will close. The Lord has mercifully spared me to a ripe old age, for if living on the 27th day of next September I shall be eighty-four years of age, and I have already been permitted to see one great-granddaughter married and attend the commencement exercises of the Chicago Musical College with another, who upon that occasion received her teacher's certificate. And I also record with thankfulness that the Lord has permitted me to occupy a desirable position in the church to which I have many years belonged, being one of what is called the " early seven," which I will here explain. During the year 1849, through death and removals, the Christian Church, for a time, was not in an organized condition, and of the few remaining, I was told, some were contemplating seeking a church home elsewhere. I then went to talk with Brother M. H. Baldwin and wife, and, being joined by Brother and Sister Saunders, who afterwards moved to Iowa, we conferred together and decided to meet the following Lord's day for worship. Accordingly, we met as we had proposed, and our number was increased by Dr. Major and an elderly brother by the name of Reese Out of this small organization (having only an earthen service pitcher, still preserved by the writer) has grown a church numbering many hundred in North, South and West Chicago. But of the original seven, only Dr. Major and myself remain identified with the present in this city. I am also happy to know that taking care of the first babies, and subsequent events, have identified me with one of the noblest institutions in Chicago,

the Foundlings' Home. And it is to me a source of satisfaction and
thankfulness that not one sick baby that I took care of while there died;
and although my connection with the home has been for nearly twenty
years principally of a business character (as Dr. Shipman always paid me
a liberal percentage, both as canvasser and collector for *Faith's Record*),
I shall never cease to pray for the prosperity of the home and its faith
workers. The little paper *Faith's Record*, which comes to "stir up your
pure minds by way of remembrance," has from year to year brought me
to your doors, a recipient of your oft-repeated and never-to-be-forgotten
kindness, for which I again thank you all, hoping this expression of my
gratitude may meet your eye when I shall have passed away. I know you
did not show kindness for the sake of thanks, yet we are all human
enough to experience pleasure in knowing that our kindness is appreciated
by those upon whom it is bestowed. Yet we may rejoice in the thought
that though we sometimes suffer from the ingratitude of others, it will prove
as nothing if only our names shall be found written in the "Lamb's Book
of Life." And let us hope that we may all be permitted to meet where
the flowers of love and gratitude are in perpetual bloom, where "the smile
of the Lord is the feast of the soul." I am not writing an adieu, for, if
the Lord permits, I hope again to look upon your smiling faces and hear
your kindly greeting. I cannot say, as did the Apostle Paul, that I have
finished my course, for I know not when this earthly tabernacle shall be
dissolved; but I do know that we have "a building of God, a house not
made with hands, eternal in the heavens," and I can say with Paul, "I
have fought the good fight; I have kept the faith; henceforth is laid up for
me a crown of righteousness, which the Lord, the righteous Judge, will
give me at that day; and not to me only, but unto all them that love his
appearing." Ladies, when I have written what I am now about to, I presume you will consider it high time for me to close this biographical sketch
of myself, but I want you to know I have already spoken with Dr. Shipman concerning my last resting-place. I said to him: "As I took care of
the first home babies, it seems to me appropriate that I should be buried
with home babies." He thought so too, and promised, if he outlived me.

he would see it arranged as I desired, and a gentleman living in Austin says if I am brought to Forest Home to stay with the babies he will see that I have a monument.   It seems to me a beautiful thought that in the morning of the resurrection I may rise, surrounded by these "little ones," " for of such," said He, " is the Kingdom of Heaven."

MRS. LAURA DICKEY, AT THE AGE OF EIGHTY-THREE.

SERMON.

Rev. J. W. Allen Discusses the Rev. Alexander Campbell and
Protestantism.

ALEXANDER CAMPBELL AND HIS WORK.

A T the West Side Christian Church the Rev. J. W. Allen preached the following
sermon:

The life of a great man is always an attractive study, and it loses none of its
attractiveness when it is connected, as the lives of great men often are, with some
great movement in history. Such lives are centers of far-reaching influences; rep-
resentatives of facts in human history; incarnations, as it were, of great truths and
principles. In studying the lives of such men, we are studying more than their lives—
we are studying the lives of myriads of our race, we are watching the development of
great principles vitally related to the well-being and progress of mankind.

The history of Martin Luther, for example, is more than the history of Luther.
It is the history of the Protestant reformation of the sixteenth century. Not that he
began that movement, for he did not; there were Protestants long before Luther's
day. All such movements come as the day comes. There is a point of time when
the sun appears above the horizon and all eyes behold it. But first there is a faint
glimmer of light in the eastern sky, then a brighter red and still brighter, heralding
the day. There were

HERALDS OF THE REFORMATION

long before Luther rose like a sun to scatter the long night of Romish darkness.
There were Huss in Bohemia, and Savonarola in Italy, and Wickliffe in England, and
all over Europe were hundreds and thousands who were hoping and longing for the
coming of the day. All these hopes and longings seemed to meet at length and
blend in Luther, and through him broke forth in one splendid protest against the
cruel superstitions of the Church of Rome. And when, October 31, 1517, he nailed
his ninety-five Latin theses to the door of his little wooden church at Wittenberg, he
fairly launched upon the world the reformation of the sixteenth century, and became

under God its leader and champion. I repeat, then, that in studying the life of Luther we are studying more than one life; we are studying the history of the reformation. We are studying a great movement which has brought up with it the destinies of myriads of our race. The same is true of the life of Alexander Campbell. It possesses an interest apart from itself. It, too, is a part of the great religious movement, and that we may know that this is well worthy of our study let us remember that

NO RELIGIOUS MOVEMENT

since the day of the Apostles ever had such rapid growth. It is only little over half a century since it was inaugurated, and yet it has outstripped in the race denominations whose history dates back more than two hundred years, and to-day only two Protestant denominations enroll more members.

God not only raises up the men who are to accomplish his purpose in the world, He also appoints their fields of labor. The Roman empire was made ready for the coming of Paul. The reformation of the sixteenth century would never have been what it was had the reformer appeared among the weak races of Southern Europe instead of among the sturdy Germans of the North. Three of the most important events of the world's history took place about the same time—the invention of the printing-press, the discovery of America and the Lutheran reformation. Luther was born thirty-five years after the invention of the printing-press, and nine years before the discovery of the New World. The art of printing most powerfully aided the work of Luther. Indeed, humanly speaking, it is not probable he would have succeeded without it. All the printers and booksellers were on the side of Luther and helped to circulate his work, whose pages

FELL FROM THE PRINTING-PRESS

like leaves from the trees in autumn, and were borne by the breezes to heaven, to every country in Europe, "and the leaves of the tree were for the healing of the nations."

When Alexander Campbell, descended from Scotch-Irish parentage, related on his father's side to the Covenanters of Scotland, and on his mother's side to the Huguenots of France, finished his education at the University of Glasgow, he was, under the providence of God, transferred to the New World. New wine should be put into new bottles. God was about to pour forth the new wine of a new religious movement, and there was a new world ready for its reception. Alexander Campbell landed in New York City September 29, 1809, and in the following year, on July 15, delivered his first discourse in Washington County, Pa. It has been regarded as singular that Alexander Campbell should have begun his preaching in the almost wilderness of the New World, rather than in some one of its great and growing seaboard cities. Had the plan of beginning been left to the election of human wisdom, it would doubtless have been some other than it was. But

GOD'S THOUGHTS

are not as our thoughts, nor His ways as our ways. When He raised up John the Baptist, He sent him not to Jerusalem, but into the wilderness of Judea. And the ministry of Jesus was carried forward not in Judea, but in Galilee, amid a simple, less bigoted and less prejudiced people than those of Judea and the Holy City. The most fruitful harvests are grown in new soil freshly broken. And the people to whom Alexander Campbell first preached were, of all others, the best fitted to receive the new message he was soon to deliver. They were the pioneers of a new nation, the fore-runners of a new civilization, the newest, freshest, richest soil of humanity, not hard-beaten beneath the tread of immemorial customs, not over-grown with the rank weeds of prejudice and superstition; but a simple-minded people, unconventional, intelligent, a brave and liberty-loving people, a people prepared of the Lord, ready to receive the scattered grains of fruit from the sower He would provide.

I once saw a beautiful water-lily growing up out of a rank and loathsome pool. When we come to study the reformation of Luther in Germany, and the

REFORMATION OF WESLEY

in England, we find they are like beautiful lilies growing up out of loathsome pools. When Luther appeared upon the scene, the Church of Rome was utterly corrupt; some of the popes had been murderers, libertines and sensualists. In 1510 Luther made a visit to Rome and saw with his own eyes the shameless wickedness of the church; saw convents full of lazy and luxurious monks; saw the priests hurrying through the mass and expressing atheistic sentiments in the midst of the most solemn services, and he carried away such an impression that he afterward said, "I would not for hundreds of thousands of florins have missed seeing Rome. If I had not seen it I might have been troubled lest I had been unjust to the Pope." The immediate occasion of Luther's attack on Rome was the sale of indulgences. An indulgence was a license to commit sin. These indulgences, like a license to sell liquor, were sold to any one who could pay the price. Tetzel, the vender of them in Germany, said: "There is no sin so great that an indulgence cannot remit; and even if any one had offered violence to the Blessed Virgin Mary, mother of God, let him pay, only let him pay well, and all will be forgiven him." The indulgence, too, was able to free a soul from purgatory. "At the very instant," said Tetzel, "that the money rolls at the bottom of the chest, the soul is liberated,   ·

ESCAPES FROM PURGATORY

and flies to heaven." When this man came to Luther's town selling indulgences, the lion in Luther was aroused, and he began his war on Rome.

The same is true of the Wesley reformation. Religion in England was at a very low ebb. A converted preacher was as rare as a comet. Religion was likened to a frozen or palsied carcass. The preaching of the Gospel had almost ceased; the sermons were moral essays; the spiritual religion was buried under forms and ceremonies. The clergy were usually sons of the gentry, and spent their time mostly in drinking, hunting and riotous living. Such was the condition of religion in England, especially in the established church, when John Wesley was born in Epworth in 1703.

The Church of Rome is a great spiritual despotism. It denies to the people the right to interpret for themselves the Word of God. One of the positions taken by Luther in his war on Rome was the right of every man to interpret the Bible for himself. This is one of the principles of Protestantism. This principle, so true and so necessary to the life of religion, may be abused. It began to be abused before Luther died.

LIBERTY RAN INTO LICENSE,

and numerous sects and denominations began to appear. Christ formed one church —"On this rock will I build my church," not churches. He prayed that His followers might be one. The early Christians were of one heart and one mind, and when divisions began to appear they were promptly rebuked. Protestant Christendom is, however, in singular contrast with this. There are scores of religious parties. Fifty years ago the feeling between these parties was bitter in the extreme. Each party strove for supremacy, each maintained its peculiarities with a zeal as ardent and persecuting as the laws of the land would permit. The distinguished tenets of each party were constantly thundered from the pulpit. They would not commune with each other; they would not attend each other's meeting, and if they did were liable to the discipline of their church. Such was the uncompromising spirit prevailing that the most trivial things would produce a division, and members were known to break off from their congregations because the preacher presumed to give out before singing two lines of a hymn instead of one, as had been the custom. Against these unscriptural divisions

ALEXANDER CAMPBELL

raised his voice, and as the Lutheran Reformation was occasioned by the corruption in the Church of Rome, and that of Wesley by the impurity and irreligion of the Church of England, so the religious movement led by Alexander Campbell was occasioned by the divided condition of Protestant Christendom.

In the year 1501 Martin Luther became a student at the University of Erfurth, then the most celebrated school of Europe. One day, as was his custom, he entered the library and opened many books to find the author's names. One volume attracted his attention. He had never until then, however, seen its like. He read the title. It was a Bible. His interest was greatly excited. His heart beat wildly as he held the divinely inspired volume in his hand. With indescribable emotion he turned its pages. He went to his room with a full heart. "Oh, that God would give me such a book for myself," he thought. He returned to the library to pore over the new-found treasure. He read it again and again, and then, in his astonishment and joy, returned to read it once more. In that Bible lay hidden the great Reformation. Just twenty years after Luther entered the University of Erfurth, where he found the Bible, he was summoned by Charles V., Emperor of Germany, to appear before the Imperial Council of Princes of the Empire to answer the charges against him. He went, and before the Emperor and Princes gave his reason for his position, first in German and then in Latin. They replied, "We want no reasons, but short answers. Will you recant? Yes or no?" Luther gave

THE MEMORABLE REPLY

"I will give an answer, an answer without teeth or horns. This is my answer: Convince me by clear proofs of Scripture and sufficient reasons, and I submit. The Popes and Councils have often erred. I can not deny plain Scripture at their command. It is not safe nor wise to act against one's conscience. Here I stand; I can not do otherwise. God help me, amen."

Luther's reformation grew out of the Bible. His appeal was to the Bible. His great work was the translation of the Bible into German. The same is true of the Wesleyan reformation. It also grew out of the Bible. Members of the Holy Club, to which he belonged at Oxford, were called "Bible moths," "Bible bigots." Wesley was anointed with the same spirit that was in Luther—a desire to live to God and to do the will of God. Luther does not belong to the Lutheran Church; no church can confine his spirit, nor appropriate his name and fame. Wesley doesn't belong to the Methodist Church, and never did.

THESE WERE GOD'S MEN,

and were His gifts to the race. They did not get all of the truths out of the Bible. Who has? But they took it for their guide and practiced what they believed it taught.

Mr. Campbell did the same thing. He opened the Bible and said: "When the Bible speaks, I will speak; when the Bible is silent, I will be silent." When Wesley studied the Bible he saw some things that Luther did not see. He did what Luther would have done—accepted them, taught them, practiced them. When Alexander Campbell studied the Bible he saw some things that neither Wesley nor Luther saw. He did what they would have done—accepted them, taught them, practiced them. The position that Mr. Campbell followed in the line of the great reformer who had come before needs some qualification. It is no disparagement to these illustrious men to say that Alexander Campbell saw with a clearer vision and a broader view than they. He lived in an advanced period of the world's history. He stood

UPON A LOFTIER EMINENCE.

The air was purer, his vision had a wider range. The question is often asked me, "How does your church differ from other churches?" I have not always found it easy to answer the questions in a few words, either to my own satisfaction or to that of the person asking it. I want to say, however, that there is a difference, a difference that is radical. And it grows out of the difference between the work that Alexander Campbell sought to do, and the work that such distinguished reformers as Luther and Wesley sought to accomplish. Luther's and Wesley's work may properly be called a reformation. They sought to reform the churches of which they were members. Mr. Campbell sought, not so much to repair defects in modern Christianity, as to restore primitive Christianity. He said, "We will go back to the beginning; we will take up the work where the apostles left it; the stream of Christianity has become muddy and unwholesome; we will go back to the fountain where the waters are pure; we will go back beyond councils and synod; we will put aside all man-made creeds and confessions and systems of theology, and sit at the feet of the Great Father and His Apostles." In following out this purpose, Mr. Campbell and those associated with him were compelled to do some things that were singular. They said: We will organize congregations of believers as they were organized by the apostles; we will give them no human name, but the name we find in the Bible. In speaking of our race there are two names, and only two, that

INDICATE UNIVERSALITY,

the name Man and the name Christian. All other names are local; all other names tend to divide; all other names lie more or less at the foundation of rival interests; but the name Man and the name Christian lie at the foundation of universal brotherhood; as men we are one in Adam, as Christians we are one in Christ. We will take the name Christian, they said, and call our congregations Churches of Christ. We will adopt no human creed and no man-made robes of government. If the creed contains less than the Bible, it contains too little; if it contains more than the Bible, it contains too much; if it contains neither more nor less than the Bible, but is just like the Bible, we have no use for it, for we have the Bible, believing "that all Scripture given by inspiration of God is profitable for doctrine, for reproof, for correction, for instruction in righteousness, that the man of God may be perfect, thoroughly furnished to all good work."

When any one asks admission into the church we will not ask him to relate his experience or subscribe to a doctrinal statement of belief, but will do as the Apostles did, question him about just one thing, his faith in Christ. "He that hath the Son hath life." In the recent Congress of Churches at Cleveland, the creed problem was up for discussion, and the question was, "How may modern creeds be so revised as to be no longer a source of discord or

DISUNION AMONG CHRISTIANS?"

Brother B. B. Tyler, representing us in the congress, made a speech on the question which was received with prolonged and rapturous applause. The solution proposed for the difficulty, seemingly new to the congress, has for fifty years been one of our hobbies; that is, "Instead of revising modern creeds, restore the primitive creed." "Believe on the Lord Jesus Christ and thou shalt be saved." The object of the faith that saves the soul is not a doctrine, however true, nor a system of theology, however scriptural, but a person, and that person the Lord Jesus Christ. Under the Ptolemaic system of astronomy it was held that the earth was the center of the solar system. As long as this was accepted as true, there were confusion and disorder everywhere. There were difficulties the astronomers could not solve; mysteries they could not unravel. But Copernicus at length announced the true order of the heavens. The sun was the center. All difficulties were then solved. Around the center the earth and all the planets moved in orderly course, each keeping time to the music of the spheres. Christ is the center of

THE CHRISTIAN SYSTEM.

Put anything else in the center and there is confusion. Take your reckonings from Him as the Central Sun, holding that trust in Him and loyalty to Him make one a Christian, and all disorder begins to disappear. If any one asks: "What must I do to be saved?" we will give the answer given by the apostles. Faith in Christ, repentance toward God and baptism into the name of the Father, Son and Holy Spirit, were the conditions upon which they promised the forgiveness of sins. We will observe the Lord's Supper every first day of the week, for this was the primitive practice. In all of our congregations there shall be bishops and deacons, for that was the divine order; and then we will call upon all Christians to unite on the Word of God, rejecting as martyrs of religious faith and practice everything for which we cannot give a "Thus saith the Lord."

In union there is strength. A hundred barrels of powder, a handful here and a handful there, fired, will burn and produce some concussion; but bring it together as they did in New York harbor, powder and dynamite, grain to grain, barrel to barrel; stretch through the whole mass the electric wire; let on the current, and there is an explosion that shakes the earth and

RENDS THE ROCKS OF HELL GATE.

God's people are a scattered people, toiling on a church here and a church there, having some power, and each doing something to bring the world to Christ; but bring them together, unite them in bonds of Christian love, and then let on the fire that comes from the touch of the finger of God, and something will have to give way. We have the promises of the Savior that the gates of hell shall never prevail against the church, but the church thus united would soon prevail against the gates of hell. "Neither pray I for this alone, but for those also who shall believe on me through their word, that they may be one as Thou, Father, art in me and I in Thee; that they may be one in us, that the world may believe that Thou hast sent me." Christian union is the need of the hour. There are forces at work in modern society not only antagonistic to Christianity, but to the order and progress of society; elements of darkness and disorder, such as

RUM, ROMANISM AND SOCIALISM,

which will ere long compel Christians to abandon their petty strifes, and their senseless divisions and unite on the Word of God, not only for self-protection, but for the order and happiness of society. God hasten the day! Two men-of-war met on the high seas. In the darkness of night, mistaking each other for enemies, they opened fire, and all through the night the battle raged. But as the morning dawned they looked and, lo! each was flying the British flag. They saluted each other and at once prepared to meet the foe that was coming down upon them. Brethren of all the churches, if we be Christians we are flying the same flag, and now in the growing light it is time to salute each other and get ready to meet the common foe, even now bearing down upon us.

A NARRATIVE.

The following narrative was related by Anthony Sherman, an octogenarian, who heard the account from Washington's own lips:

" The. darkest period of our Republic was the year 1777, when Washington, after experiencing many reverses, went into winter quarters at Valley Forge. Often I observed tears course down the cheeks of our beloved commander when he was considering the sufferings of his brave soldiers.

" Washington was in the habit of praying in secret and calling upon God for assistance, and it was only by the help of God we passed safely through those days of adversity.

" One day Washington spent the whole afternoon in his room alone. When he came out I observed that he was much paler than usual, when he related to me the following:

Whilst I was sitting at my table this afternoon, engaged in writing, and my mind heavy with sorrow, I suddenly observed directly opposite to me a most beautiful female.

He was Surprised.

I was so much surprised, for I had given strict orders not to be disturbed, that I could not find words at the moment to enquire the object of this unexpected visit. Two, three, and even four times I repeated the question without receiving an answer, the only effect being that she raised her eyes a little. I now experienced a most curious sensation spread over my whole body. I wished to rise from my seat, but the steady gaze of my mysterious visitor kept me spellbound. I again tried to speak to her, but my tongue was tied. An unknown, mysterious, irresistible power had taken me prisoner. I could do nothing else but steadily gaze at the apparition. Gradually the room filled with light, and the form grew more clear and bright. My feelings were those of a dying man; I could neither think nor act. My steady gaze at the figure was all I was aware of. I now heard a voice which said: "Son of the Republic, behold and learn!" At the same time the figure stretched out its arm and pointed with the finger toward the East. Light clouds arose in the distance, which dispersed and revealed to my eyes a most astonishing picture.

All the Earth.

Before me all the countries of the earth were spread out—Europe, Asia, Africa and America. Between Europe and America I saw the waves of the Atlantic Ocean toss backward and forward, and between America and Asia the waves of the Pacific Ocean.

Again I heard the voice: "Son of the Republic, behold and learn!" Immediately a dark form like that of an angel appeared over the ocean between Europe and America. It then dipped water from the ocean with both hands, and with its right sprinkled it over America, and with its left over Europe. Immediately dark clouds arose from both of these countries, which met in the middle of the ocean; here they remained stationary for a while, then moved westward and wrapped America in darkness. Lightning flashed through the dark clouds, and I heard the groaning and the shrieking of the American people. Again the angel dipped water from the ocean and sprinkled it as before. The black clouds withdrew and sank into the sea.

Saw America.

For the third time I heard the voice: "Son of the Republic, behold and learn!" I looked toward America and saw populous villages and cities from the Atlantic coast to the Pacific Ocean. Again I heard the mysterious voice: "Son of the Republic, the end of the century is near at hand. Behold and learn!" The dark form of the angel then turned toward the South, and coming from Africa I observed a horrible phantom making its way to our country. It floated slowly and heavily over our towns and the country; the inhabitants arose to make war on each other, and formed in

battle array. As I looked at this scene I observed an angel surrounded
with light; on his head he wore a beautiful crown, on which was inscribed
the word "Union." In his hand he held the American flag. This he
planted between the contending armies, crying out: " Remember you are
brothers!"

Immediately the nations threw away their arms, became friends again,
and gathered around the flag.   .

Heard a Voice.

Again I heard the mysterious voice: "Son of the Republic, the second
danger is past. Behold and learn!" And I saw villages and cities steadily
increase in size and number until the whole country was covered with
them, the whole extent, from the Atlantic to the Pacific Ocean, and the
nation had multiplied in as countless numbers as the stars in heaven or the
sands on the sea shore. Again I heard the voice: "Son of the Republic,
the end of the century is at hand. Behold and learn!" The dark angel
then put a trumpet to his mouth, blew it three times, then dipped out some
water from the sea with his hand and sprinkled it over Europe, Asia and
Africa. My eyes now beheld a most terrible scene. From each of these countries dark, heavy clouds arose and united in one mass; through this mass
dark red lightning played. I saw troops of armed men advancing, and
then sail across the sea to America, which was immediately covered by the
black cloud. And I saw how these immense armies desolated the land and
laid towns and villages in ashes. I heard the roar of cannon, the clashing of
swords, the cry of the victorious and vanquished millions engaged in
deadly strife; when again I heard the mysterious voice proclaim: "Son of
the Republic, behold and learn!" The dark angel then took up the
trumpet and gave one long and terrible blow. Suddenly a light burst forth
and drove away the dark cloud hovering over America. At the same time
I saw the angel with the beautiful crown, on which was inscribed the word
"Union," descend from heaven, holding in one hand the Star Spangled
Banner, and in the other a sword, and accompanied by legions of heavenly
spirits. These united with the American people when the latter were

almost overpowered, and they took fresh courage and formed in battle array. Again, amid the horrible noise of war, I heard the mysterious voice: "Son of the Republic, behold and learn!"

For the Last Time.

After this voice the dark angel dipped out water for the last time from the sea and sprinkled it over America, and immediately the dark cloud retreated with its armies, which it had brought along, leaving the victory to the Americans.

I then again saw towns and villages rise in the same places where they had stood before, while the heavenly angel planted the Star Spangled Banner among the people with a loud voice: "As long as the stars are in heaven, and as long as the dew descends from heaven to earth, so long shall this republic exist." .

At the same time he took the beautiful crown from his head, on which was inscribed the word "Union," placed it on the Star Spangled Banner, and, kneeling down, cried out, "Amen!" The apparition then appeared before me in my room, and again I heard the voice: "Son of the Republic, what you have seen is explained as follows:

The Close.

"Three dangers will come over this republic. The second is most to be dreaded. When this one is past the whole world cannot conquer her. Let every child of the republic learn to serve his God, his country and the Union."

With these words the form vanished. I arose from my chair with the conviction that the birth, progress and fate of the United States of America had been revealed to me.

"These words," says Mr. Sherman, "I heard from General Washington's own lips."

We know that the first two sections of the vision have been fulfilled. The last is now upon us. The reason for so vivid a picturing of the future of this country before him was because he needed a strong re-assurance from

some quarter. He had come to where he could not be pacified with the
ordinary helps of his mind's reasonings or his religious convictions.

REMARKS OF NAPOLEON I, CAPTIVE OF ST. HELENA.

In the course of a few years Russia will have Constantinople, part of
Turkey and all of Greece. This I hold to be as certain as if it had already
taken place. All the cajolery and flattery that Alexander practiced upon
me was to gain my consent to effect that object. I would not give it, fore-
seeing that the equilibrium of Europe would be destroyed. In the natural
course of things Turkey must fall to Russia. The powers it would injure,
and who would oppose it, are England, France, Austria and Prussia. Now,
as to Austria, it would be very easy to secure her assistance by giving her
Servia and other provinces bordering on Austrian dominions, reaching near
to Constantinople. The only hypothesis that France and England will ever
be allied with anything like sincerity will be to prevent this, but even this
alliance will not avail.

France, England and Prussia united cannot prevent it. Russia and
Austria can at any time effect it. Once mistress of Constantinople, Russia
gets all the commerce of the Mediterranean, becomes a great naval power,
and God knows what may happen.

The object of my invasion of Russia was to prevent this, by the inter-
position between her and Turkey of a new state, which I meant to call into
existence as a barrier to her eastern encroachments.

Turkey will not long serve as a wall between Russia and the Mediterranean. Any rectification of the map of Europe that accepts Turkey as a
breakwater to the waves of Russia's ambition will prove worthless. The
Moslem has served his purpose. He has done his work, and, wasting daily,
he must soon pass away. The great sacrifices made from 1854 to 1856 to

preserve Turkey have served only to exhaust and waste her. " Weighed
and found wanting, and given to another" is her doom.

Among the many methods employed by Russia in her pursuit of un-
limited dominion, two are remarkable. They are practiced chiefly toward
her less civilized and less powerful neighbors.

One is to keep a body of Russian troops by friendly agreement in the
territories of some other state, serving that state and receiving its pay
for a given period. The other is to raise a force, and this also in an amica-
ble and preconcerted manner, among the inhabitants of a foreign contermin-
ous region, to draft that force into Russia, to maintain it with Russian
money, and to incorporate it more or less permanently with the Russian
army.

Both of these expedients have, respectively, important effects. The
first teaches the Russian soldier everything that a future invader might
find it necessary to learn of the resources, manners, temper and geographi-
cal condition of the people amid whom he is thus temporarily domesti-
cated. He notes the weak points and the strong, and hereafter can clearly
show to his government what should be avoided, what may be seized, what
precautions are requisite; what opportunities exist, how the whole work of
occupation should be managed. He is making a long reconnoissance, and
on a grand scale. More than this, he is becoming acclimatized.

In the other case, where Russia levies a foreign body, drafts them into
her territory and pays them, equal effects are produced. They are not like
those Russian troops of whom we have just spoken, and whom the Czar
loans to a neighbor now and then; they are not, like those troops, dis-
ciplined soldiers, still under orders of their own officers, and those officers
carefully selected, holding constant communication with their own country,
changed and replaced at will.

No! they are foreign troops commanded by Russian officers. They are
troops who are taught and drilled in Russia, who are under control of
Russia, and who see only just what she pleases. When Russia withdraws
her auxiliary contingents, she withdraws spies; but when she disbands her
other class of troops and sends them back to their own land, she sends back

emissaries, agents and proselytes, who prepare the way in their simple homesteads for the coming of the double-headed eagles under which they have served, and for the coming, moreover, of some old comrade in high command, who, perchance, having displayed superior abilities, has been promoted and induced to naturalize himself in Russia, and to accept the allegiance of a state which loads him with crafty and insidious distinctions.·

Doubtless the disbanded and returned troops could teach their countrymen something of the defenses of Russia, in the same manner as the Russian contingent can give the converse information.

But terms are not equal. There is no question even of invading Russia among those feeble communities; but in Russia their invasion or absorption is a business quite within practical realization and duly predetermined.

This double system has been long pursued by the huge despotism of the East all around its lower frontiers—from the shores of the Caspian and of the Azof, down to those of the Black Sea—among all the tribes of the Caucasus who could be brought into that dangerous intercourse, and among the dependencies of Persia.

WOMAN'S WORK.

MRS. J. E. CHACE.

From the Mishawaka Enterprise.

What is it? The answer given to this inquiry by the "Lords of Creation" has become stereotyped. That woman must marry, cook her husband's dinner, iron his shirts, tidy the house and wash the children's faces has, we think, been conceded ever since Mother Eve took her first lesson in housewifery. And we were willing— oh, how willing!—to intrust all that pertained to the public good to those who were accounted our superiors. And had they as faithfully discharged their duty when considering the public weal as did woman in the daily routine of domestic life, then, indeed, it might not have become necessary for her to step out of the pre- scribed limit into a wider field of action. But, alas! There came a day when it dawned upon woman's feeble intellect that something was amiss; that those to whom she had blindly confided the interests of this great commonwealth had either ignorantly or designedly betrayed the trust reposed in them. The evil which in its incipiency had been overlooked, or willingly ignored, had been permitted to assume gigantic pro- portions; brooding like a bird of ill omen until, like a pall, it overspread and darkened the fair face of civilization; blighting and destroying all who succumbed to its evil power. And she whose home had been the sweetest, holiest spot on God's green earth found herself thrust out; her children beggared; and she, together with them, made the victims of such cruelty as only a drunken husband and father would inflict; and to her dismay she found for all this there was no redress; for the same evil presence polluted our halls of legislation and defiled the lowliest hut; and with blanched cheek and quivering lip she prayed (for I had forgotten to mention that this privilege had been granted her in addition to those already named), prayed oh how earnestly, that He who sitteth upon the throne might pity and assist her in this terrible emergency, and seeking consolation in His word, she read, "Faith without works is dead, being alone." Thus were the eyes of her understanding opened, and, endeavor- ing to walk the divinely appointed way, she has since "shown her faith by her works." Although in the performance of this necessary work we find ourselves hedged about and circumscribed, yet we hear the precious voice of the Master saying, "She hath done what she could." We are not discouraged because we have not been able in a short space of time—with hands tied—to unravel all the intricacies which the sterner sex have spent years in weaving, but, working patiently on, we are enabled to offer the prayer of faith, which asks deliverance from this monster, which finds no place too high or too low for his occupancy. And we know that God hears us. "For the trumpet now is sounding that shall never know retreat until the demon of strong drink is crushed beneath our feet." But fathers, husbands, brothers, sons, this great work rests measurably with you. Will you be found among those who come up to the held of the Lord against the mighty? If so, well; if not, remember God reigns, and He will devise ways and means of working out this social problem without your assistance. May God speed the work of prohibition! ⟨ W. C. T. U.

THE W. C. T. U., HAVING CUT THEIR EYE-TEETH, WILL NOW ABANDON THE SOOTHING-SYRUP POLICY.

Mrs. J. E. Work.

From the Enterprise.

"She hath done what she could" was the commendation of the divine Teacher as the penitent woman kneeled at His feet and washed them with her tears. His promise was that it should be a memorial of her for all time; and through the ages women have wept and prayed, not only in penitence for their own sins, but more often in behalf of fathers, husbands and brothers. But the time has come when weeping and praying will not avail. The deadly serpent of the still is dragging his slimy folds over the sacred precincts of our homes, lifting his hydra head and hissing in our ears his horrible purpose to destroy our most cherished hopes and blast our dearest expectations. And shall we sit tamely by and do no more than weep and pray while our loved ones are being slain before our eyes? Is this all we can do, or shall we take the advice of one of our legal gentlemen in a speech at one of our street temperance meetings? He advised the praying brothers and singing sisters, as he called them, to enforce the laws that they have, giving it as his opinion that they are sufficient to protect us if enforced; as if we do not understand the perfect farce of trying to enforce law against business licensed and protected by law! Thank you, gentlemen. Women may be very illogical, but they are not fools, and we will leave the soothing syrup now to teething children. We have cut our eye-teeth, and do not need it, but we are not going to abandon the field to the enemy by any means. We intend to keep this matter before the people. Miss Frances Willard, in one of her speeches, said that the letters W. C. T. U. had two other interpretations in the work of the different organizations, all tending to the same end. It means we come to unite, and in our efforts to suppress the traffic it means we come to upset, and this we intend to do. And may the great Ruler of the universe strengthen our hearts and lengthen our tongues, and, taking prohibition for our watchword, we will sing in the ears of the voters of this Republic till from very weariness of hearing it they will avenge us of this our adversary by voting to stop the manufacture of this liquid fire and brimstone, which is the first as well as the second death. And as faith and talk will not do without work, do not be alarmed if you see some of the singing sisters coming toward you with a collection card, but smilingly put your hand in your pocket and furnish the needful dimes which we must have to carry on this work. Mothers, sisters, rouse yourselves to the importance of the work before us, and help to drive this evil from our land, and then will come the time of which the angels sang on the plains of Judea, "Peace on earth, good will to men." W. C. T. U.

THE RIBBON OF BLUE.

MRS. JULIA E. CHACE.

Mishawaka, Indiana, April 12, 1881.

Young man, what would you not do for the mother
  Who loves you as only a mother can love,
Who would e'en give her life, could she save you from sinning,
  And for you ever pleads with the Father above?

Would you banish forever dark clouds of foreboding,
  Bring joy to the heart ever loving and true,
Let me whisper it, boys, this and more you'll accomplish
  By fearlessly donning the Ribbon of Blue.

Not a true-hearted sister, wife, maiden or mother
  All over this fair licensed whiskey-cursed land
But devoutly thanks God when her loved or another
  Resolves in the strength of true manhood to stand.

Then haste thee to flee from the death-dealing billows,
  Which ruin and blacken as onward they roll;

Flee! flee from the wine whose deadly aroma
  Will wreck and destroy thee, both body and soul.

Aye, boys, with pride wear the " badge " as a token
  That unto yourselves you will ever prove true,
That the vows you have spoken shall never be broken
  And your lives pure and true as this Ribbon of Blue.

DAVID AND THE GIANT IN 1882.

MRS. JULIA E. CHACE.

As backward we tread in the annals of time,
A prominent city named Gath we may find;
There sunbeams danced brightly over valley and hill,
And sweet flow'rets bloomed by the murmuring rill.
But, 'mid balmiest breezes, with beauty surrounding,
Was Goliath, the giant, spreading terror around him.

To the armies of Israel his challenge was sent,
Twice repeated each day, until forty were spent
In defying the leaders of Israel's host
And vaunting his prowess in blasphemous boast,
'Till, dismayed and disheartened, they return no defiance;
Must they yield to this power unwilling compliance?

No! a man, small of stature, and only a youth,
With right for his might and his armor of Truth,
Walks forth, in the name of the Lord of Hosts,
To meet the bold giant and silence his boasts;
For helmet and breastplate, sword, spear and shield
Can no longer give safety—his doom is now sealed.
Armor, prowess and strength prove alike unavailing ;
  *   *   *   *   *   *   *
For their champion slain, the Philistines are wailing.

Friends, we've many Gaths of modern date;
They abound and flourish in every state
Where a hydra-headed giant is found
Spreading death and destruction all around ;

His armor is kept without rent or flaw,
For 'tis made of the liquor-license law.
E'en the pure air from heaven by his breath is polluted,
And the ruin he's wrought has ne'er yet been computed.

Worse than thousand Goliaths, this whiskey fiend's boast ;
For his victims each day are a countless host.
And shall we idly stand while this monster destroys
The hope of our nation, fair girls and brave boys?
No! like David, who met and conquered the foe,
In the name of the Lord of Hosts we'll go
Armed for the contest ; and thus may we live
'Till Israel's God shall the victory give.
For on Thee, oh Lord, do we place our reliance ;
Thou can'st wholly defeat, tho' 'twere legions of giants.

ALABASTER BOXES OF HUMAN SYMPATHY.

Do not keep the alabaster boxes of your love and tenderness sealed up until your friends are dead. Fill their lives with sweetness. Speak approving, cheering words while their ears can hear them, and while their hearts can be thrilled and made happier by them; the kind things you mean to say when they are gone, say before they go. The flowers you mean to send to their coffins, send to brighten and sweeten their homes before they leave them. If my friends have alabaster boxes laid away, full of fragrant perfumes of sympathy and affection, which they intend to break over my dead body, I would rather they would bring them out in my weary and troubled hours, and open them, that I may be refreshed and cheered by them while I need them. I would rather have a plain coffin without a flower, a funeral without a eulogy, than a life without the sweetness of love and sympathy. Let us learn to anoint our friends beforehand for burial. Post-mortem kindness does not cheer the burdened spirit. Flowers on the coffin cast no fragrance backward over the weary way.

GENERAL GORDON.

[General Gordon, just before leaving England for the Soudan, sent a message to Canon Wilberforce, ending, " I am now calmly resting in the current of His will."]

BY WILLIAM LUFF.

It is easy when the current bears us softly through the vales,
Where sweet music ever cheers us and sweet fragrance fills the gales;

Where the sunlight gleams upon us and the flower-banks shield from harm,
It is easy to be restful when the stream is hushed and calm.

But it dashes and it crashes, and the rocks oppose its course,
As it rushes through the chasm with a wild, impetuous force;
Lo, it leaps in foaming fury o'er the cataract's dark brow!
Am I resting in the curreut? Am I calmly resting now?
Trust it, brother, ever trust it, for it cannot lead thee wrong ;
Never dare to stem its progress, for its power is wise as strong ;
Though it wind among the mountains, where the shadows darkly fall,
Calmly rest upon its bosom, trust its majesty through all.

Do its waters overwhelm thee ? Art thou troubled and distressed ?
Carried onward, carried downward, all is working for the best.
Hold the centre of the current, shun the rocks of human craft ;
Calmly rest upon its bosom, and no hurt shall reach thy raft.

I am resting, calmly resting, in the current of His will ;
Where it bears me I am happy, be it cataract or rill;
Like a straw upon the waters, I would yield myself to go
Just wherever He shall bear, and rejoice to have it so.

I am resting, calmly resting, in the current of His will ;
Not a struggle, not a murmur, in the whirlpool restful still.
O, delightful, sweet submission! O, enjoyed and perfect rest !
Till I reach the boundless ocean and His loving, peaceful breast.—*The* [London]
    Christian.

IO VICTIS.

W. W. STORY.

I sing the Hymn of the Conquered, who fell in the battle of life—
The hymn of the wounded, the beaten, who died overwhelmed in the strife;
Not the jubilant song of the victors, for whom the resounding acclaim
Of nations was lifted in chorus, whose brows wore the chaplet of fame—
But the hymn of the low and humble, the weary, the broken in heart,
Who strove and who failed, acting bravely a silent and desperate part;
Whose youth bore no flower in its branches, whose hopes burned in ashes away,
From whose hands slipped the prize they had grasped, who stood at the dying of day
With the work of their life all around them, uplifted, unheeded, alone,

With death swooping down o'er their failure, and all but their faith overthrown.
While the voice of the world shouts its chorus, its pæan for those who have won—
While the trumpet is sounding triumphant, and high to the breeze and the sun
Gay banners are waving, hands clapping, and hurrying feet
Thronging after the laurel-crowned victors—I stand on the field of defeat
In the shadow, 'mongst those who are fallen, and wounded, and dying—and there
Chant a requiem low, place my hand on their pain-knotted brows, breathe a prayer,
Hold the hand that is hapless, and whisper, "They only the victory win
Who have fought the good fight, and have vanquished the demon that tempts us
      within ;
Who have held to their faith, unseduced by the prize that the world holds on high;
Who have dared for a high cause to suffer, resist, fight—if need be, to die."
Speak, history ! Who are life's victors? Unroll thy long annals and say—
Are they those whom the world called the victors, who won the success of the day?
The martyrs, or Nero? The Spartans who fell at Thermopylæ's tryst?
Or the Persians and Xerxes? His judges, or Socrates? Pilot, or Christ?

DIED.

Lilly May, infant daughter of Albert and Anna Kellogg, was born August 2, 1873, and died September 28, 1874.

TO MR. AND MRS. KELLOGG.

Like a beautiful sunbeam, bright and fair,
Came your babe to bless and your love to share,
But O how dark and dreary the day
When she like a broken lily lay!

We knew, as we noted the failing breath,
That very near was the angel of death;
But we felt that redolent grew the air
With the white rob'd messengers ling'ring there.

We wept o'er the anguish witnessed when
Was severed the bud from the parent stem;
But, leaving the chill, bleak shores of time,
Transplanted, it blooms in a lovelier clime.

As we gazed on the waxen form so fair,
And severed one tress of shining hair,

Then closed the beautiful eyes so blue,
Not lost, we murmured, for well we knew

Though the footfall here wakes echo no more,
Firm is its tread on the golden shore.
There, blest in the light of His love, she waits,
'Til for thee shall be opened the pearly gates.—MRS. JULIA CHACE.

IN MEMORIAM.

(Addressed to Mr. and Mrs. Potter on the death of little Truman.)

A priceless treasure to thee was lent,
  Which day by day more beautiful grew,
'Til hope and love wove visions bright
  Of the future years of baby Tru'.

Time sped on, and the rosy lips
  Lisped the music of accent sweet,
While an added joy to the parent heart
  Was the echoed patter of little feet.

Love environed, he grew apace,
  But, ah! life's numbered years were few.
For His treasure lent the Father sent,
  And the angels hasten'd for little Tru'.

How doubly blest are the early called
  Eternity's years can only unfold,
For the Shepherd there gives tenderest care
  To the precious lambs of the "Upper Fold."—MRS. J. E. C.

THE WARNING DREAM.

"GOD LOVETH A CHEERFUL GIVER."—COR. IX: 7.

(The following lines were suggested by the perusal of a story in which was given a vivid description of the different views entertained by a husband and wife regarding the true aim and object of existence. She, possessing a practical faith which mani-

fested itself in works, truly believed when she "gave to the poor she lent to the Lord,"
and endeavored to "do His commandments, that she might have right to the Tree of
Life, and enter through the gates into that city where gold finds no place, save in the
formation of its streets, 'neath the tread of the redeemed." He, time-serving and
void of sympathy, recognized no obligations outside the precincts of his own luxurious home—for he represented that numerous class who stop at no expense inasmuch
as it contributes to their own happiness, but for any other purpose cannot be induced
to part with their "shining gold." Upon one occasion—after denying his wife the
privilege of carrying into effect some benevolent design—he fell asleep over his paper
and dreamt that death, having first robbed him of his loved ones, had at last brought
him into the spirit world, where, through a land dark, lone and dismal, he was has-
tening to join the loved ones who had preceded him. His disappointment and the
cause will be found embodied in this poem.)

He dreams, and lo! through the mystic realms
    Of the valley of shadows he wends his way;
    Still presses he on with an eager tread,
    For beyond where sunset glories are shed
Lies the beautiful city of endless day.

Onward, for oh! how he yearns to greet
    His loved and lost who have gone before;
    He knows, just beyond those battlements bright,
    The glory of God and the Lamb is the light,
And fain would he dwell on that radiant shore.

Ah, see! a gleam of that wondrous light
    Now pierces the shadows which brood o'er his way;
    'Mid the rivulets pure and meadows green
    Of that bright beyond forms belov'd are seen.
Oh, the bliss of re-union in endless day!

Poor man: so near, yet so far away
    From his shining ones in the love-light pure;
    He—on the barren so bleak and cold—
    Sees rising a wall formed of glittering gold,
More bright than of yore, still it fails to allure.

"Lost, lost!" he wails, and the echo resounds
    Through the length and breadth of that desolate land.
    See! a swift-winged messenger, robed in light,

Like a vision of beauty bursts on his sight.
List the cry: "Comest thou with a helping hand ?"

Though his glance told how great was the pity of heaven,
  Still firm the response by this Son of Light given:
  "Not for thee bloom and beauty or exquisite song,
  For this golden obstacle, high and strong,
  By thy hand erected, must evermore stand,
Forbidding thine entrance to yon blissful land.

"No heed wouldst thou give to His promise or love,
  Who fain would have built thee a mansion above.
  O fatal decision, devotion to self,
  And insatiate greed of this glittering pelf,
  Which sparkles and towers and dazzles for thee!
Of thy sowing, behold, this the harvest shall be!

"Oft thy chosen companion tearfully plead
  That thou would'st give to the famishing bread.
  Thy response, 'What folly it is to suppose
  In striving to lessen humanity's woes,
  We lend to the Lord, who with treasures untold
  Will repay this improvident outlay of gold;
  Better keep what we have; I think it more wise
Than this effort by *proxy* to build in the skies.'

" 'O husband,' she wailed, ' 'tis madness to scoff,
  For the earth is the Lord's, and the fullness thereof;
  His the cattle upon a thousand hills,
  And shall we refuse to dispense as He wills?
  Like an eye of flame burns the changeless Word:
  ' He gives to the poor who would lend to the Lord.'
  Though wretched and lowly the suppliant be,
' Thou shalt thus,' said the Master, ' bestow upon Me.'

"Thus, day by day, as the years were enrolled,
  Rose the mansion fair, by her sweet faith controll'd.
  And the gold *she* lent on that love-illum'd street
  Laid the shining pavement beneath her feet;
  Thine, garnered and treasured by thy command,
  Built this golden structure, massive and grand;
  'Tis all thine own, yet this barrier of thine

Shall exclude the light of the inner shrine—
Withhold from thy sight and fond embrace
Treasured form and angelic face.
Thine, ever thine, it shall glitter for thee,
For time-chosen treasures eternal shall be!''

MRS. JULIA EWER CHACE.

Mishawaka, Ind.

JESUS OUR REFUGE.

MARK IV : 37, 38, 39.

Wildly the tempest swept over the sea,
'Til but upheaving billows was deep Galilee;
Thrilling the cry 'bove the mad waters' rave :
'' We perish ! we perish !— Lord hear us and save ! ''

Though gently was spoken that '' Peace, be still,''
Winds and waves bow to His gracious will ;
Again do the depths mirror perfect respose,
As the blue wave in peace and tranquillity flows.

E'en thus, O our Savior, we cry unto Thee,
As wildly we're toss'd on life's perilous sea,
And our frail bark shrinks from each pitiless wave ;
We perish ! we perish ! if Thou dost not save.

Oh, for that faith which shall lead us to Thee,
Though "walking the waters" of life's troubled sea ;
Nor let us sink down 'neath its treacherous wave ;
Lord, help us !—We perish if Thou dost not save.

From the waves that o'erwhelm—of sin and regret—
From the evils which ever our paths here beset ;
From all that sheds darkness or gloom o'er the grave,
O Lord, our Redeemer, defend us and save.—MRS. J. E. C.

MARY.

WRITTEN BY REQUEST.

More sweet than the breath of Araby's bowers,
  Wafting afar on orient gales,
Kissing the morn whose wealth of bright hours
  More radiant grows as the future unveils:

Aye, dearer and sweeter than combining aromas
  Distilled from the heart of exotics most rare,
Is the fragrance emitted by mem'ries which cluster
  'Round the Marys, so gentle, devoted and fair.

Like a strain of sweet music from harp-strings Æolian,
  Floating along through the dim aisles of time,
Comes the record of purity, love and devotion
  Which e'er round the Marys of old must entwine.

That "better part" by a Mary was chosen;
  "Mary's tears bathed His feet," pride and vanity gone;
"Last near the Cross" 'twas a Mary who lingered;
  "At the sepulchre Mary was seen with the dawn."

O'er the brow of one evermore "bless'd among women"
  Is woven a chaplet of bright immortelles,
And down through the age with the sweet name of Mary
  A charm never fading and potent still dwells.—Mrs. J. E. C.

DEDICATED TO MY SCRAP BOOK.

BY MRS. JULIA CHACE.

Dear silent companion, thy pages are rife
With the purity, sweetness and beauty of life;
From thee may we gather the sweet echo chime
As softly it floats down the dim aisles of time,
'Til, wrapt in its melodies, rich and rare,
Life woos us anew with its freedom from care.

In thee do we find, exquisitely wrought,
Purest gems, won from the bright realms of thought;
And still shall they shine, while the ages shall roll,
With rays that refract, reproduce in the soul
Emanations sublime, which here to us given,
Prove a foretaste sweet of a sinless Heaven.

When I shall have pass'd to the other shore,
May these sweet exotics I've lingered o'er,
By my dear ones sought, rebloom in the heart,
And their rich fragance to them impart.
Thus shall utterance pure with harmonies blend,
And only with time may its mission here end.

TO MR. AND MRS. F. G. P.

'Tis said the weather on the bridal (as bride's) day, and the succeeding one (groom's day) indicates or omens the kind of life the newly-wedded shall lead together.

May the untried years of thy future prove
Bright and serene as the bridal hour,
Illum'd by the light of a deathless love,
Controll'd by the light of its magical power.

If perchance but a shadow may seem to obscure
The beautiful light of that rose-tinted realm,
Bear and forbear is a talisman sure
To open the flood-gates of radiance again.

E'en thus may the bark of the twain made one
Securely float down the river of time,
'Til, bathed in the splendor of life's setting sun,
Entranced thou shalt list to the evening chime.

And still where the ages of time shall merge
In eternity's fathomless, limitless sea,
Beyond the knell of a parting dirge,
May thy love continued perfected be.—MRS. J. E. CHACE.

JENNIE LIND.

The following lines were written more than forty years ago, shortly after Jennie
Lind came to America.

I have listened oft with pleasure
  To the praises, loud and long,
Lavished in no stinted measure
  On the beauteous Queen of Song.
Oh! how much I've longed to share
In listening to that voice so rare.

By a noble mind attended,
  I have thought this voice was given
By His love, who, though ascended,
  Grants a foretaste of that Heaven,
Where the good, the pure, the free
Join their sweetest melody.

As one drop from out the ocean
  Is the semblance given here
Of that blissful, thrilling portion
  Granted in a holier sphere,
Where the myriad voices sing
Anthems to their Savior King,

May the yet unrivalled songstress
  To earth's sons be given long,
Gladdening by her gift so boundless,
  Cheering by her glorious song.
May she, when from earth set free,
Join the angels' minstrelsy.

To her heart, so pure and gentle,
  Be the shield of mercy given,
Fitting it for its presental
  To that glorious home in heaven,
Where sweet praise is ever hymned,
May'st thou be welcomed, Jennie Lind.—JULIA E. CHACE.

THE OLD BRIDGE.

Chant me a requiem sad and slow,
No more shall I gaze on the ebb and flow
Of thy silv'ry wavelets, old St. Jo.

Ah, well, I am told, whether lowly or great,
All things earthly must meet their fate,
And mine, 'tis apparent, is to " cremate."

Twenty odd years I have served full well,
And while in your midst am permitted to dwell,
Treasured secrets would scorn to tell.

Though such, indiscreetly, I may not promulge,
In reminiscence I fain would indulge
And my own meditations thus divulge.

Flitting like dreams through the shadowy past,
Memories varied crowd thick and fast,
Soon, oh soon, they will prove the last.

Trembling, and wearied with labor and time,
To a younger and stronger I soon shall resign,
And gladly the care-freighted future consign.

Thrilling anew, I remember the hours
When the beautiful earth seemed a garden of flowers,
And love's whisper sweet, as neath sylvan bowers.

I remember, too, with grief and pain,
Oft the frenzied cry, which proved but vain,
Of bleeding hearts in the funeral train.

In politics, too, I became well versed,
As from year to year, with insatiate thirst,
I listened to hear the subject rehearsed.

The grand old flag, our national pride,
I have seen imperil'd when treason defied ;
More firmly it waves since its subjects were tried.

Beautiful words of praise I recall,
Ascending to Him who reigns over all ;
But oh ! with what terror, what dread, what appall,

E'en wooden ears shrank from the language profane
With which men in their madness their souls still stain.
"Thou My name," saith Jehovah, "shalt not take in vain."

The inebriate's song I've heard with disgust,
And marveled that one with so holy a trust
Could the glory of manhood thus trail in the dust.

Would that the words that Divine love hath given
Home to the hearts of offenders were driven,
"No drunkard can enter the Kingdom of Heaven."

Many lessons hath life, oh, heed while ye may,
For darkness must follow the sunniest day,
And on all things is written "Passing away."

Then chant my requiem, soft and low,
One lingering farewell glance bestow,
As I to the land of oblivion go.

BLUES.

My subject, though gloomy and chilling—the blues—
Since named by my husband, I may not refuse,
Though I'd fain with a happier theme be impressed
When thought assumes form and to him is addressed.

Should this investigation prove prosy or dry,
Perchance prompt reproof—a frown or a sigh—
I trust you'll forgive, or at least will excuse—
Inspiration itself must needs die near the blues.

"What's the matter, my dear," is a query not new,
As the visage elongate is presented to view;
A voice—from its tone might proceed from the shoes—
Replies, "Nothing, nothing, only I've got the blues."

Answered, I grant; still must I muse
O'er this manifest sadness styled briefly "the blues."
The cause? asks my heart; oh, why need this be?—
Trembling the while lest 'tis traced back to me.

Repents he the vows which our lives thus entwined?
Have I proved less constant, devoted or kind,
Than anticipation, when wandering through
Misty lands of the future, presented to view?

He says to this "No;" "What is it then, pray?"
"'Bothered, perplexed, and discouraged' you say;
I feel that 'tis true; still, this do you know—
Where the rose-bloom is fairest, the sharpest thorns grow?"

"Were there here no perplexities, sorrow or strife,
Who would e'en give a thought to that holier life?
Were the soul aspirations, the spirit's glad trust,
Like the clay that enshrines, they'd be wedded to dust."

"Then let us, dear husband, with cheerful content,
Bear the darkness and clouds which in kindness are sent;
Though luxuries may to us be denied,
Let us limit our wants by subduing our pride.

"Thus, when cares pale the cheek, and years dim the eye,
We'll remain young in spirit, for love cannot die;
Then, with hope weaving o'er us his tri-colored hues,
We'll banish forever these heartaching blues."—MRS. J. E. C.

RECIPE.

I WISH, for the benefit of mothers, to say I discovered, while taking care of sick babies, that Sea Moss Farina was a very valuable article if properly prepared. Bennie Grout would soon have died with the canker and indigestion which had taken possession of him if something had not immediately reached his case. I took of Sea Moss Farina one teaspoonful, one pint of boiling water, a pinch of salt, also of sugar; put all together in his bottle and let him drink all he wanted between times of nursing—never, be it remembered, oftener than once in three hours. And the same preparation can be used with one pint of milk added and all boiled together, to give young babies as food, as there is a mucilage in it which keeps the milk from curdling in the stomach. This food is particularly adapted to weak stomachs, but care must be taken to follow the directions, as more than I have named of the farina in its proportion would produce too frequent evacuation.

www.ingramcontent.com/pod-product-compliance
Lightning Source LLC
Chambersburg PA
CBHW032355020726
47499CB00008B/2755